My Husband Simon

Mollie Panter-Downes

BRITISH LIBRARY

First published in 1931

This edition published in 2020 by
The British Library
96 Euston Road
London NW1 2DB

Cataloguing in Publication Data
A catalogue record for this publication is available from the British
Library

ISBN 978 0 7123 5312 0
e-ISBN 978 0 7123 6756 1

Text design and typesetting by JCS Publishing Services Ltd
Printed and bound by CPI Group (UK), Croydon, CR0 4YY

Contents

❦

⋇ ⋇ ⋇

The 1930s

⋇

⋇ Between 1930 and 1935, unemployment rates in Britain average 18 per cent.

⋇ **1931:** *My Husband Simon* is published.

⋇ **1931 (April):** The first Highway Code is issued in the UK.

⋇ **1931 (October):** Ramsay MacDonald remains Prime Minister in a landslide victory for the recently formed National Government, but he is expelled from the Labour Party.

⋇ **1932 (October):** Oswald Mosley founds the British Union of Fascists.

⋇ **1935 (July):** The first Penguin paperbacks go on sale, costing sixpence each. This gave the masses cheap access to literature, and three million were sold within the first year. The non-fiction imprint Pelican Books follows in 1937.

⋇ **1936:** The Carnegie Medal is inaugurated, awarded to writers for children or young adults. The first winner is Arthur Ransome, with *Pigeon Post*.

⋇ **1936 (October):** The Jarrow March sees 200 men march from Jarrow, Tyneside to London, in protest against unemployment levels.

❦ ❦ ❦

❦ 1936 (**December**): Edward VIII abdicates after less than a year as king, so that he can marry divorcée Wallis Simpson.

❦ 1939 (**November**): *And Then There Were None* by Agatha Christie is published (though under a title now considered racist). It will go on to be one of the bestselling novels of all time.

※ ※ ※

Mollie Panter-Downes (1906–1997)

※

Mollie Panter-Downes was born as Mary Panter-Downes on
25 August 1906, and was only 8 years old when her father was
killed in action in the first month of the First World War.

Her first novel was published in 1923, when she was
only 17. *The Shoreless Sea* – the tale of naïve and romantic
Deirdre – sold very well, with reviewers commenting that
it showed a maturity beyond her years ('nothing of the
clever schoolgirl about it'; 'it is not a work of precocity'; 'a
remarkable achievement for its girl-author'). She followed it
up with *The Chase* in 1925 and *Storm Bird* in 1929. By the time
My Husband Simon appeared, she had gained a husband of her
own: she married Clare Robinson and moved to Haslemere,
Surrey, where she would live for the rest of her life. Robinson
changed the name of their house from West End to
Roppelegh's, after its fifteenth-century owner, Richard de
Roppelegh.

In 1938, she started a writing relationship that would
last for almost half a century. Her first piece for the *New
Yorker* appeared despite discouragement from her agent, and
she would contribute over 850 stories, articles, poems, and
letters. During the Second World War, Panter-Downes was
the voice of England (and more particularly London) for
many Americans, writing detailed fortnightly letters on the

＊ ＊ ＊

situation across the Atlantic. While these included politics, each provided an account of everyday life, from queuing to bus services. She continued her 'Letter from London' into the 1980s.

For many years, it was for this form of journalism that Panter-Downes was best remembered. In recent years, more of her fiction has been republished. Her remarkable post-war novel *One Fine Day* (1947) has been recognised as a modern classic, and her *New Yorker* short stories have found a new audience. She lived long enough to see some of this reappraisal happen, dying in January 1997, survived by two daughters and a lot of excellent writing.

※　※　※

Preface

※

My Husband Simon was Mollie Panter-Downes' fourth and
last pre-war novel before she turned her focus to short stories
and journalism. Though reflective of its time, referencing the
servant problem for instance, it still has something to say to
a contemporary audience about the position of women, the
complexity of relationships and the desire for self-expression.
Furthermore, amid the ambivalent emotions and the difficult
choices, there are sharply observed, sensual descriptions of
smells and vivid evocations of place.

My Husband Simon begins with the narrator, Nevis
Falconer, in New York in 1930 looking back on her first
meeting with Simon Quinn, when she was just 21, and the
intense physical attraction which led to their tempestuous
marriage. To the reader, Nevis might seem the central
character but the title reflects her description of Simon as the
dominant figure in her unwritten book.

Throughout the story, in autobiographical echoes, Nevis
is struggling to reproduce the freedom and success of her
first novel. There is much about the importance of writing,
of needing the space, independence and opportunity to
write. *A Room of One's Own* had been published in 1929 and
a knowledge of Virginia Woolf is one of Nevis's tests of
intellect. There is a strong element of (partly acknowledged,

❧ ❧ ❧

partly satirical) intellectual snobbery in Nevis's attitude to literary taste and she foreshadows Betjeman by several years in her description of Slough. Yet while Nevis to some extent compares intelligence unfavourably with intuition it is Simon – whose lack of interest in books and reading is contrasted with his father's bibliographical enthusiasms and the well-read Marcus Chard – who predicts that Nevis will have left him before their 10-year pact of town-living is up and who first articulates that Marcus, her American publisher, is in love with her.

The novel reflects many of the themes of the period such as the fear of change felt by some and the desperate longing for change endured by others. Nevis experiences an overwhelming sense of suffocation, both literal and psychological, in the stifling heat and in the company of her in-laws, and is contrasted in this by her more acquiescent sister-in-law Gwen. Many people will recognise her feelings of restriction and limitation and her attempt to overcome them.

Alison Bailey
Lead Curator Printed Heritage Collections 1901–2000
British Library

My Husband Simon

I

❦

New York. Autumn, 1930.

I sometimes wonder, looking back at everything with the experience that four years ought to have brought, whether I would make up my mind quite so precipitously to marry Simon Quinn if I met him for the first time to-day. There are moods in which I tell myself: "Not a hope! Freedom and work are the only important things. My God, haven't four years taught you anything at all, you damn little fool?" But at the back of my head I know quite clearly that if it happened all over again I should marry Simon just the same. I could yell and scream; I could run away to some place six weeks from Southampton by a fast boat. Running would only bring me back to the inevitable fact, like one of those dreams in which you tear out of a room in a crazy, nameless panic, and find yourself back again where you started.

London four years ago—more than four years, really, for it was at the end of a scorching week in July. Over here they laugh at English summers, but that week had seemed like something angry, slowly gathering and throbbing to a white-hot head. In the late afternoons I went into the Park and sat limply on the grass by the Serpentine; the trees on the other side looked unreal and a little distorted, as though a sheet of hot glass were stretched between them and me. Even the pavements seemed to sweat. At night you saw people strolling with linked arms, and pale, relaxed faces that reminded you of those starry kinds of flowers that only open up in the cool of the evening.

It was the week-end of the Eton and Harrow match. The streets were full of small boys walking about behind haystacks of cornflowers; cars were tied up with pale-blue ribbons like cart-horses at a country fair. I had been up to the ground with Roddy Talent on Friday and had walked round, eyeing the other women's clothes until a rather nice pair of Hanan shoes were grey with dust and hurting me like the devil. It was all rather stupid, rather pointless, very charming, unmistakably British. I remembered that Soames Forsyte had gone to Lord's and had seen Irene there in a dove-coloured dress. The thought quite cheered me; at that time Galsworthy was my god. I don't suppose that I watched more than a couple of overs.

On Saturday I was going down for a short week-end to the Fentons' at Burnham Beeches. The thought of getting away from the smell of hot pavement and hot people was rather nice; still, I packed in a bad temper. Mrs. Proutie, my charwoman, had not turned up that morning to get my breakfast. I lived in a tiny flat with bright yellow walls and a geyser as temperamental as a *prima donna*. Proutie got my breakfast; then I settled down and worked until I got hungry, when I either dug up some biscuits and went on working, or else ran round the corner to a little restaurant. The same little restaurant supplied my dinner, unless some man took me out. Quite simple, you see, when it worked. Unfortunately, Proutie was like the geyser, temperamental. I couldn't rely on her, but she was always cheerful, and, so far as I could see, didn't steal the gin.

That morning I had made coffee and sliced a grape-fruit for myself, rather peevishly. The explosion of the geyser nearly threw me out of the bathroom and broke two cups on the dresser of the kitchenette next door. Already it was hot. I dragged out my suitcase and started to pack, half my mind occupied irritably with a short story that had been worrying me all the week. It refused to sparkle or to come alive; although I was generally the most cordial admirer of my own work, something seemed to tell me: "This is wasting your time—burn it!" Skin food, a yellow crêpe sports suit, tan-and-white shoes—but supposing I look at things from her point of view?—how many evening dresses do I want? Only one night. I looked unenthusiastically at a black chiffon, and stuffed its flounces with tissue paper. ... Perhaps I've fiddled with it so long that it's gone sour on me. Perhaps I'd better burn it. Oh, damn! ... There was only just time to catch that train.

Slough is the station for Burnham Beeches. Even in a good temper I dislike Slough. That morning it seemed to me a town without a single excuse for itself; a foul industrial blot spreading slowly over those pleasant fields towards Windsor. I wondered what kind of people could possibly wish to live in Slough, and pictured men with faces on which avarice and pettiness of soul were stamped like mean handwriting on cheap paper; women who made fumbling, ineffectual gestures and said "Pardon!" when they committed a social error. I wondered how many people in Slough had ever heard a Beethoven Symphony or seen a Leonardo.

My dislike of the unfortunate place was so absurdly vindictive that it almost put me in a good temper again. As I got out I saw the neat dark-blue figure of Shelby, the Fentons' chauffeur, trotting up the platform towards me.

"Hallo, Shelby!"

"Good-morning, miss. Let me take your suitcase. The car is just outside, miss."

Shelby was a great friend of mine. The car, an enormous pre-war Daimler, was the absorbing pride of his life. When you asked him how his wife was doing, Shelby would say: "Wonderful, miss. We've only just had her decarbonised, and she's running like a bird. I keep telling Mr. Fenton we ought to have her painted, but she'll do as she is till spring, he says."

I liked the Fentons' house. It was Georgian, red brick with cream-coloured doors and windows; its lines were unpretentious and satisfying. A big magnolia tree grew up the side of the dining-room window, and in it were perched three flowers like creamy, snug-bosomed birds with faintly pink throats. Frank was fond of his garden. In autumn these borders blazed with dahlias and straggling, lavish Michaelmas daisies, so that the heart was warmed on the most melancholy day; now that it was hot yellow summer there were clouds of white phlox, and delphiniums so pure and cold a blue that they were like strange flowers grown in a glacier. ... London seemed a very long way off.

The front door was open. I walked into the hall, and stood pulling off my gloves. It was cool and dim. On the centre table there was a quantity of lavender drying on newspapers. I could see through the morning-room into the garden and hear voices and the sharp, irritable ping of tennis-balls.

"They're all down at the courts, miss. I'll fetch Mrs. Fenton."

"No, don't bother. I'll go down."

I started to walk slowly across the lawn. There were two or three people sitting in wicker chairs under the cypress. The players had just finished a set; someone was struggling into a sweater. Cora cried: "There she is!" and darted to meet me.

"My dear, it's so lovely to see you!"

Cora had a funny, breathless way of speaking, as though she could not trust her attractive husky voice to hold out for long. I loved her. I suppose that she was the best woman-friend I ever had; on the whole I did not care for women. She was thirty-five, ugly in a fascinating way, with no colour at all in her small face or her beautiful *cendré* hair, which was uncut, swathed tightly as a turban round her head. Her ankles were lovely. Chanel dressed her. She had three ugly *cendré* children and was supposed to love Frank Fenton, which I thought distinctly unenterprising.

"I'd better go and change, Cora."

"No, darling, it's nearly lunch-time, and anyway you look adorable. Come and meet people."

I glanced towards the group on the tennis-court.

"Are they all staying here?"

"No, only Simon Quinn. I don't think you've met him here before. Simon!"

Frank came over, his face red and glistening.

"Hallo, Nevis. You look damn cool. Been to Lord's?"

"Yesterday afternoon. Don't ask me what the score is—I haven't the faintest idea."

"You girls only go to look at each other's clothes."

"Frank, darling, you read us like a book."

Simon came over. He was the young man whom I had noticed struggling into a sweater.

"Nevis, this is Simon Quinn. Nevis Falconer, Simon."

He had curiously light eyes with dusty gold lashes. I thought, "He's attractive." I felt suddenly angry and helpless, as though I knew that the nice, orderly little pattern of my life was going to be broken up. He said:

"I wish that I could say I'd read your book."

"Why should you?"

"Well, it would make a good beginning. But, as a matter of fact, I don't read anything. I'm practically illiterate."

He made the statement with an irritating satisfaction. Cora slipped a hand under my arm and took me away to say how-do-you-do to people. The butler came carefully over the lawn carrying a tray of cocktails. I sat down next to a woman who fixed her eyes on my feet and demanded:

"Do you live in London? I suppose that the sarvant problem is a good deal easier thar than it is har?"

Thinking of the criminal Proutie (she would have to clear up all the mess that I had made packing, and serve her right, old cow), I answered wildly, "Far, far more difficult," and saw that Simon was watching me, smiling.

❦

Simon Quinn.

I wonder how to describe him. He was short, not much taller than I was, but I never saw anyone better-built. He had good features: a straight nose; rather small, stubborn mouth; wilful chin. His hair was the dusty gold of his lashes, and those lashes were the laziest in the world. They drooped perpetually; the whole eyelid seemed to droop, giving him a peculiar secret sort of expression. He was twenty-eight, and on the Stock Exchange.

This made me laugh. I could not picture him in a black coat and striped trousers, running after a 'bus. He ought to have lived in the country and kept horses and a lot of dogs. He hated a town. That was where we disagreed, for although my people had lived in Gloucestershire for centuries, I had the love of a town right in my marrow. I adored a lot of movement and new contacts and the sense of something doing. Before I ever thought of coming here New York attracted me because it was a city built on the sea and always changing; great mushroom growths of steel and concrete shooting up overnight; big liners coming and going. I used to like the idea of lying in bed at night and hearing them go "*Wham! Wham!*" from the harbour.

Simon, I discovered almost at once, was the most baffling person to deal with, because he had any amount of intuition and no intelligence, as I understood the word. But Simon argued once that I understood the word all wrong. He said that I damned anyone as unintelligent who (*a*) had not seen the latest play and read the latest novel; (*b*) did not know who Virginia Woolf was; (*c*) could not look at a dress and say, "My dear, is it Molyneux?" Well, Simon certainly failed in (*a*), (*b*) and (*c*). He never read books; he didn't give a damn who Virginia Woolf was; he thought a dress was either a bad dress or a good dress; and that was that.

On the other hand, he was as uncannily intuitive as an animal—as attractive as an animal, too. You wanted to touch him as you might want to touch a dog who was enjoying life, or a stallion bright with physical well-being. Before the end of that first evening at Cora's I knew that I was in love with him, and was wondering what in hell to do about it.

There were guests to dinner. It was so hot that we were discussing, rather listlessly, the prospects of a thunderstorm. We dined with the long windows wide open; moths drifted in and queer little red things with hard, thin bodies that dashed themselves furiously at the candles. Cora, in white with a huge square emerald on her left hand, was talking to Simon and making him laugh. I turned to Frank, and entered into a passionate discussion on the right soil for lupins, a subject which is hardly one of my favourites. When I looked Simon's way again he was not laughing, but watching me under his lids; a strange, speculative look.

Someone put on the gramophone. We danced for a bit. I have tried, but I can't remember the tunes. Simon came and sat down beside me.

"I want to know all about you."

"That sounds alarming."

"I've got a bit out of Cora. You're twenty-one. You live alone. You've written a book. Is it a bad book?"

I said rudely: "Yes, very."

He looked as though he believed it. I was furious. He asked: "Have you any family? What are they like?"

I paused to consider my family. Both my father and mother were dead. My father had been killed in a hunting accident when I was five; I hardly remembered him at all. A photograph showed grey eyes like mine and the same broad, square forehead.

My mother had died only two years before. She was an amazing character. We quarrelled continually. Irish blood had given her great vivacity and a strong streak of superstition which she confused with theology in the most blandly humourless way. When I found a horse shoe she took it to be a sign that God loved me. I have seen her carry a lump of coal for miles— coal was another sign of a beneficent providence. She used to write the names of all the Grand National runners on bits of paper and draw them out of a wash-basin; oddly enough, the animals chosen in that way either came home in a canter or fell dead at the starting-point.

I had living a grandmother and an aunt, both in Gloucestershire, and various uncles and cousins. Granny was my father's mother. When we went to see her as children she used to ring a bell and the whole pack of us had to come running, wherever we were or whatever we were doing, as quickly as possible, if we didn't want our knuckles rapped. Everyone was terrified of her. She was in love with the family doctor, and used to get him into her room on the flimsiest pretexts. The two would sit telling stories and eating bull's-eyes that Granny kept in an enormous jar beside her bed. I went up to stay with her once a year. Her invariable greeting was: "Well, Nevis, your neck's dirty and there's too much paint on your mouth. Come and kiss me." I wasn't really fond of her.

I looked at Simon and said firmly:

"All my family are quite negligible."

"That's good."

"Why?"

"Well, it makes things less complicated, doesn't it?"

I couldn't or wouldn't see what he meant. I wanted to get away from this cool stranger who was threatening the neat little plan of my life. That was quite clear from the beginning. I knew that if I married Simon I should have to fight hard for my work and my individuality. His personality was so strong that it might swamp me. Already I knew that he was obstinate and ruthless; that he liked very few of the things that I liked, and was ignorant as a savage about everything that I had been taught to respect. The thought of our life together appalled and fascinated me. I looked at him and thought: "But intellectually you are much weaker than I am; I could always get the better of you that way."

For a moment this comforted me; I felt foolishly snug and superior. Simon had been looking out into the garden, where Cora was strolling with someone. Her white dress flickered. She called: "Frank, bring the cigarettes out. We're being chewed to death by these damned bugs."

Simon looked back at me. His face was hard and unsmiling as though he had been thinking the same kind of thoughts. "Who is this Nevis Falconer, anyway? What the hell does she want to come pushing into my life for? She'll only make trouble."

We looked at each other in silence. Everything went out of my head. I only knew that Simon attracted me enormously and that I attracted Simon enormously. I didn't even know if he would want to marry me. He might want me to live with him, and in that case I should live with him. But there was going to be something. It wasn't just a casual meeting at a week-end party. ... Good-bye. Nice to have met you. Ring me up sometime.

Simon, looking at me angrily, said:

"I didn't know that you'd be like this."

The next day we were idle. It was too hot to do anything strenuous. We just lay about in the cool, leafy places of Frank's garden, listening to the ice-cubes tinkle in our glasses. Cora was not one of those hostesses who harry their guests by feverishly organising things for them to do. She curled her funny little body into a deck-chair and went to sleep like a cat.

I lay dozing, sunk in a queer sort of stupor of contentment. Nothing seemed to matter. Yesterday I had given birth to something strange and exhausting; now I was enjoying all the sensuous languors of convalescence. "What must come will come"—I remembered poor Tess. It seemed a nice, comfortable bit of philosophy to fall back on. The scent of hot lime-flowers was like honey. I thought of London and the flat with a shudder.

Simon and I left after dinner. He had to be in the city at nine the next morning, and I wanted to start work early on the damnable short story. He was going to drive me up to town. I felt that we were already married; our suitcases sat connubially together at the back of the car. It was a rather old and shabby Bentley.

"Are you going to be warm enough?" asked Simon. "It's quite cool."

"Oh, yes. This tweed is thick."

He did not seem to want to talk. I took off my hat and lay back and thought. It was a strange, quiet sort of evening, beautiful and rather uncanny. There was no moon. Here and there in Burnham Beeches cars were parked, and people were lying about on the grass, quite silently. Their pale faces were turned towards each other or else stared blankly up at the leaves; their bodies touched or were flung face downwards, motionless as puppets with broken legs.

When we got out on the Bath Road, Simon turned the car right, not left. I said stupidly:

"But this isn't the way to London!"

Simon explained in an absorbed voice:

"I know a little pub not far from here, on the river. I thought we might go there and have a drink first. What do you think?"

"All right."

I think that I slept. The air was so soft on my face and in my hair; it smelt of warm grass and summer and the sweetness that rises out of the earth when night comes. I wished that we weren't going to stop for a drink. I wanted to drive on when it was really dark and there were stars … to drive on … to … drive … on. …

I got out sleepily, picking up my hat from the floor. The little pub was low and white, with shutters that looked black in the twilight. There were three tubs filled with marguerites, beyond them, a half-crescent of lawn curved down to the river. I could hear a weir.

Simon said:

"There are chairs down there. I'll go and beat up a waiter. What do you want?"

"A Tom Collins."

"Right."

He went off. I saw him walk into the little hall and stand for a moment looking at a stuffed salmon in a glass case. I turned away and walked down to the water's edge. There were more marguerites, and wicker chairs and tables. It was so quiet that the distant dip-dip of oars sounded clear as crystal. I could hear a rowlock rattle, and then the scrape of dry grasses as some small, urgent wild thing pushed through them. The river smell was overpoweringly sweet and rotten.

> No sound but the boom,
> Of the far Waterfall like Doom.

But of course Simon didn't read Belloc. I must tell him about Miranda. He would like it.

> Do you remember an Inn, Miranda?
> Do you remember an Inn?

I laughed, and saw Simon walking across the lawn. He came up to me and took me violently in his arms. His mouth was hard and hurt me. The world seemed to stop. But my brain did not stop. Sometimes I hate myself because, whatever happens, I can never stop thinking. Was it Thomas Browne who wrote something about "a second man within who mocks at me?"

The second woman within me mocked:

"Well, you're both sensual. You're both egotists. He wants his way and you want yours. Run away while the running's good."

I closed my eyes and thought: "Oh, go to hell!"

Simon drew a long shivering breath and said in a queer voice: "Nevis."

"Simon."

"Damn! here's that bloody waiter."

We sat down, and I discovered how difficult it is to drink a Tom Collins when the glass is shaking. It went on shaking. I felt as though I had been in an express train and someone had put on the brakes very suddenly. Simon said:

"I can say things to you that I couldn't say to other women. You've got some sense."

"Go on. Damn this glass!"

"I think I want to marry you. Is that how you feel about me?"

"Yes."

"I didn't mean to marry for years. It will upset all sorts of plans."

"Well, what about me?"

I felt rather indignant. I thought of a scheme for a year in Paris that would have to go. Simon wouldn't like Paris. It struck me that already I was adjusting my life to take in this stranger. I looked at the dark, well-balanced outline of his head and shoulders with antagonism and fear. It was so strange to think of adjusting things to suit someone else. I was used to being independent and pleasing only myself.

"All right. Don't let's quarrel already." He laughed. "God, how we're going to quarrel!"

"Are we?"

"Like hell. And you know it. Does it worry you?"

"Not much."

"You attract me more than any woman I've ever seen. You attract me so much that I wonder if I'm not mixing up marriage with going to bed."

"It's been done before."

"I know. What's the use of talking a lot of damn polite nonsense? I don't want us to be so crazy to sleep together that we go and get tied up for life."

He got up and walked restlessly about. It was an irritating trick that I had noticed at the Fentons'. He couldn't stay five minutes in a chair. I sat and watched him. I couldn't get the boom of the far Waterfall like Doom out of my head. Boom—doom—boom. In a minute I should have to tell Simon.

He stopped abruptly, and said:

"Will you stay here for the night with me?"

Boom of the far Waterfall like Doom. So Simon was to be my Doom. But I had known that from the beginning, really. It was like coming into a dark room, and click! someone put on the electric light.

"As a kind of experiment, you mean?"

He nodded.

"You think that will make us sure?"

"Have another drink."

"No."

"Listen, Nevis." He walked away, came back again, and said: "I think I would like to marry you more than any woman in the world. But I'm not going to do so just because you've got a lovely body, and I'd like very much to sleep with that body."

It sounded funny put that way, like the report of a murder trial. Where was the body found? The body was found, my lord, on Wimbledon Common, half-clothed, and in a battered

condition. Why is it always Wimbledon Common, anyway? …
I wanted to laugh. I felt excited and reckless and happy.

"Is that the only reason, Simon?"

"Yes. The chief one. Isn't it yours? Tell me honestly."

"Yes." I laughed.

"Thank God you're honest. Well, let's get all that over. Then
we can say, 'Yes, I didn't make a mistake; I still want to marry
you.' Or just, 'It's been a good show—ring me up sometime.'"

"Thanks for the buggy-ride."

"Yes, thanks for the buggy-ride."

He turned round and stood looking at the river. He had a
curious knack of becoming suddenly and passionately absorbed
in something quite different from the business on hand. I had a
feeling that he had slipped away from me and was thinking of
that stuffed salmon in the hotel lounge.

"Simon."

I got up and put my hand through his arm.

"Do you really think that it's going to be 'Ring me up
sometime'?"

"No."

"Neither do I. I'll stay."

"I'll go and ask that damfool waiter if they've got a room."

But I kept my hands clasped round his arm. I felt suddenly
insecure and young. I wanted him to kiss me again and make
me feel that nothing mattered.

"Simon."

"Yes?"

"All right. You'd better go and get the suitcases out of the car."

He said in a low, teasing voice:

"You won't want very much for to-night."

"All the same, my dear, I think that you'd better fetch them."

We were suddenly quite wild and gay. Simon had these mad-dog moods, especially after a fit of depression; they were enchanting, and made you feel that you were assisting at something exciting and reckless like walking a tight-rope. We went into the little pub arm-in-arm. Luckily it was rather off the beat of all the lovely young men and women who hang round Cookham and Bray. In the lounge there was an engraving of Victoria receiving some bishops; a copper pan full of pinks; the salmon—a nasty, supercilious-looking fish; two quiet middle-aged men in tweeds, who were smoking pipes and drinking beer. Simon asked them to have some more with us. We all became quite friendly, and Simon told two rather funny stories.

I had never seen him before with men. He was sitting low in his chair, legs straight out in front of him, flushed, and enjoying himself. I think that he had forgotten all about me. It was a completely new aspect, and made me feel amused and tender. He seemed suddenly, not a baffling man with a horrible power to disturb me, but a childish and uncomplex creature whose knowledge of life was far more primitive than my own. Simon would have fitted in quite happily, with no conscious efforts at readjustment, if he had been put back three thousand years. Civilisation had only made possible the things he hated—towns; striped trousers; talking pictures—and had taken away all the things that he liked—the country; animals; a life that contained a certain amount of danger and required a certain amount of initiative.

I watched him and thought: "Two days ago I didn't know that you existed," and it struck me as comic that I didn't know where he lived, or who his father was. Suddenly he gave me a quick, hard look under his lids, and set down his beer-mug. No, he hadn't forgotten that I was there. Far from it.

One of the nice quiet men asked:

"Going to turn in? Well, good-night. It's been a pleasure to meet you and your wife."

Our bedroom must have been on the side nearest to the weir. The monotonous roar was loud but rather soothing. There were lighted candles on the chest of drawers and by the bed. I undressed slowly. It didn't seem, somehow, a time for doing one's face with cold cream. I looked at myself in the speckled mirror and thought how bright-eyed and strange I looked. And I had had the temerity to write a book, to try and understand men and women, when this had never happened to me before. ...

"God, you're lovely! ... Nevis, is this the first time?"

"Yes."

"I'm glad. It's the same with me."

"You're ragging." I laughed as though he had said something funny. My friends looked upon chastity in men as a subject for indifferent jokes.

"No, I'm not. I mean it."

Creaks and voices outside—our nice beer-drinking friends going to bed. I lay and looked at a funny smoky patch on the low ceiling; someone must have been careless with a lamp. Simon said:

"Let me look at you, you pretty thing." Suddenly he frowned and asked: "Why do you do such damsilly things to your eyebrows?"

"Because I want to. Don't ask questions. Oh, Simon, I love you."

The darkness seemed to come with a soft roar, in waves breaking, dissolving, breaking again. There was a rhythm to them like music. In that music one could drown. One could drown with streaming hair and sealed eyes, if suddenly an appalling tremor had not shaken the universe; the universe began to tremble; to vibrate with the thudding and monotonous sound that the weir made as it poured into the quiescent river.

> Do you remember an Inn,
> Miranda?
> Do you remember …?

Presently it was quiet. The noise of the weir seemed to have retreated. I suppose that we slept.

⁂

I let myself into the flat at eleven o'clock the next morning. Simon had not kept his nine o'clock appointment in the city. On the floor were flung-down garments and tissue-paper. Saturday's grape-fruit rinds and dirty coffee-cups stared me in the face. The bedroom had the sordid, sluttish air of a room in which the bed has not been made.

I thought of various ways of slinging Proutie out on her ear when she eventually condescended to turn up. I sat down and stared at the empty half of a grape-fruit. At any rate, the milkman had not played me false. It might be a good idea to make coffee. On the table was a pile of manuscript; I turned it over vaguely as though it belonged to someone else.

Presently the telephone shrilled.

"'Lo!"

"That you, Nevis?"

"Yes."

"This is Simon."

"Yes."

"Well?"

"Oh, Simon, my darling. ..."

II

⁂

We had been married over three years. We lived in a little house in Montpelier Place. One end was very slummy: children made chalk and other marks on the pavements all through the summer evenings, and women scurried out of the public-house carrying jugs under their aprons. On Saturday nights there was often the sound of singing and loud, quarrelling voices. Simon liked this; I think that sometimes he wanted to join them. His idea of real enjoyment was sitting in a hot, crowded tap-room, talking horses with a drunk navvy who might later try to pick a fight with him.

But our end of the street was changing. All the little houses had been re-painted; the windows were hung chastely with beige net, and one or two had window-boxes of gay metal flowers. (The neighbourhood cats, who had not shared in the refining process, were rude with real ones.) The front doors were painted scarlet or jade-green. Quite often rich-looking cars stood outside them. It was rumoured that in one of the houses there was a basement cocktail-bar, all American cloth, with walls covered in modernistic posters, and this made us rise superior to the scurrying women with their jugs and their tired, anxious faces.

The house in Montpelier Place was the result of a compromise between Simon and myself. At first he wanted to live in the country, near enough to come into town and the office every day. I hated the idea. London was in my bones; all my friends were there. But I couldn't stand up to Simon when he looked at me in a certain way, and I would have given in eventually if, with one of his sudden disarming reversals, he had not done so first.

"All right. I'll live with you in a town for ten years, and then you'll come and live with me in the country. What about it?"

He actually drew up an absurd document on the back of an old envelope, and I signed it. Simon's breast-pocket was always full of envelopes on the back of which were written cryptic things that no one could read, least of all himself.

I wanted to take another flat. Mother and I had always lived in flats; I liked the sociable feeling of being among a lot of people, and cramped space only seemed to make the rooms more friendly. But here Simon won. He thought that in a flat he would feel shut in. His horror of being shut in almost amounted to claustrophobia. Sometimes I would wake up and find that he had put on a coat over his pyjamas and gone for a walk, to get rid of a frightful sensation that he was being trapped, stifled by the four walls pressing in on him. He was really very like an animal, something wild and reddish like a stag or a fox. Occasionally one felt the faintest compunction for getting him into this cage with its neat front door and h.-and-c. laid on.

We took Montpelier Place. Sometimes I looked at it and thought how attractive it was; at other times I had fits of black gloom and wanted to smash the furniture. In reality, it was exactly like the home of every other young married couple we knew. I could have walked into the Kirkpatricks' little house in Walton Street, or Oonagh and Bryan Hardy's flat in a mews off Park Lane, and, except for the varying shape of the rooms, I shouldn't have known the difference.

Most of the walls were painted bright yellow, like the old flat. Everyone seemed to have given us lamps for wedding presents, and when these were lighted the place really looked quite attractive. I had an Italian painted dressing-table. There were the usual amount of old maps stuck on waste-paper baskets and old prints stuck on umbrella-stands, and everyone who hadn't given us a lamp seemed to have given us glass. Montpelier Place was shaken to its foundations periodically by loud and sinister crashes.

On the ground floor two rooms had been knocked into one and painted reseda-green. In the back I worked at a large desk (William and Mary, rather bad copy). In the front there was a sofa with piles of jade and apricot cushions, and over the fireplace hung the Flemish tulips and peonies that had been Cora's wedding-present.

Cora had showed no surprise when she heard that Simon and I were going to be married. Sometimes I thought that she had made a pretty shrewd guess as to how that week-end at Red Court had ended. But she said nothing, and I said nothing. If I had been going to tell anyone, it would probably have been Cora with her funny crooked smile and understanding eyes; but I had told no one. Neither Cora nor I was the type of women who confide all the more intimate details of their insides, their confinements and their beds.

Shelby drove her up to town at least once a week, and quite often she found time to come and see me. She brought me masses of flowers from Red Court; delphiniums and dark purple Canterbury bells in summer; in the autumn chrysanthemums with their spicy scent and savage ragged heads. They looked gorgeous standing about my green room.

One day Cora said suddenly:

"I think people who ask questions are perfectly damnable, and now, having settled that, I'm going to ask you one. How are you and Simon getting along?"

This was after we had been married three years. I lit a cigarette and thought for a minute.

"Cora, don't ask me. I just don't know. Sometimes it's heaven, and sometimes it's hell—everything's so muddled up that I just don't know."

Cora said swiftly:

"Who's the best man in town for tonsils, do you know? We've decided that the time has come when Michael must part with his."

Dear Cora.

❧

It was half-past six on an April evening. I had just knocked off work. On the window-sill stood a square glass jar of the daffodils that Cora had brought when she asked "How are you and Simon getting along?" They were five days old, and quite dead. Katie never thought of changing the water, and I was always too preoccupied to remember, but they must really be thrown out to-morrow. Simon, who passed through his dressing-room like a tornado that left a trail of ruined white ties and gaping cupboards in its wake, had a nasty finicky habit of jumping on things like that.

He would be back soon. The year after we married he had left the Stock Exchange and gone into the advertising side of a firm that made cigarettes, and seemed to hold out chances of better money. All our friends were in jobs like that—some rather worse. Hugh Ellerby, who had been at Eton with Simon, was traveller for a firm that made electric "Ladies" and "Gentlemen" signs. One of my cousins was trying to get a job as a sort of glorified bell-hop at the Savoy. He could speak three languages perfectly, and had great charm of manner. Well, London was full of young men who could speak three languages and had even more charm of manner. I suppose that Simon was lucky to be drawing a fairly good salary for planning advertising campaigns that gave a pair of (bad) silk stockings to anyone who collected twenty-five Mellow Cigarette coupons. If you collected a hundred coupons you were given a gold-plated toothpick, or else let off smoking Mellows for the rest of your life—something like that, anyway.

I stuffed all my papers into a drawer, feeling chilly, stiff round the shoulders, and depressed. My eyes hurt me. I looked at myself with cold disfavour in a small Venetian mirror that hung in the back room, and thought grimly:

"You're twenty-four now. Go on like this, my dear, and you'll be blind and round-shouldered by the time you're thirty."

But I knew that even the thought of being blind and round-shouldered would not put me off. I was twenty-four, and already work was a grinding relentless habit. Sometimes I used to try and imagine what it felt like to be Oonagh or Kay Kirkpatrick, who filled their days with bits of shopping, bridge, women's lunches at Sovrani's, or some place like that. I couldn't imagine. There were times when I indulged in a little easy self-pity because I was not Oonagh or Kay; because I was impelled by this ruthless, capricious force to write down things on sheets of paper and tear them up again; to labour on, stumbling and cursing and hoping. But in my heart I did not really pity myself. Some days I was numb with failure, and Simon said: "You're in a damn bad temper this evening;" other days something in my brain said "Now!" and out of the waiting silence poured words in a singing, sparkling cascade.

This had not been one of the other days.

I heard Simon's key rattle in the front door. There was a pause while he looked at the letters that were waiting for him in the hall—two bills and a circular promising to pay best prices for gents' cast-off clothing and false teeth. Then he came up two stairs at a time, calling "Nevis!"

Simon was thirty-one. In the last year his neck and shoulders had thickened very slightly. It made him better-looking, but he was exercising like mad to get the few extra pounds off again. He said: "When you put on weight, and you're tall—that's all right. But when you're not particularly tall they begin calling you a fat little man, and, my God, that's terrible."

I was sitting at my dressing-table. I watched him in the glass, not turning, as he came into the room, pushed some underclothing off a chair and sat down. He was looking bad-tempered, which meant that he was tired. Fatigue never had the effect of dimming Simon's peculiar physical quality; he had a steely reserve of strength that enabled him to go on without moving a muscle until he dropped. But he would look increasingly angry, the lid of his left eye would droop more and more; he would retreat into one of those passionately absorbed silences that shut you out with the finality of a bolted door. Presently, if you left him alone, he would unbolt the door and come forth jauntily, gay and quite enchanting again. I understood him pretty well by now.

He said:

"I've got a head like a top. Any aspirin in the house, Nevis?"

"In the corner cupboard. Don't upset all the bottles and things. You haven't forgotten that we're dining with your family to-night, have you?"

He groaned.

"Jesus, so we are."

I felt just about the same way. Dining with the Quinns was not my idea of a stimulant after a depressing day. Our periodical family gatherings always gave me the sensation that I couldn't breathe, that all the life and intelligence were being slowly crushed out of me by these terrible people. While I sat decorously eating saddle of mutton at the big mahogany table, I would have a crazy, panic-stricken longing to spring up and rush away from everyone—even from Simon, because he too was a Quinn. The phrase "a Quinn" had come to symbolise a whole class of society in my mind, just as Galsworthy uses the phrase "Forsytes" and Sinclair Lewis "Babbits." London was full of Quinns, eating saddle of mutton at handsome mahogany tables; going up the steps of good clubs and stepping out of quiet, expensive cars; thinking that "art" meant the Royal Academy, and "beauty" was the sort of wishy-washy, rubber-stamp, damnable prettiness that you see on the lid of a chocolate-box. The scent of their Sunday dinners rose from the areas of all the best residential localities. Empires might fall, men die horribly every minute, Christ come to earth again. The Quinns' Sunday dinner scented the air of the London squares, and will continue to scent them while Rutland Gate stands.

Why did I hate them? I don't know. Looking back now, it all seems so ferociously young, such a waste of energy. They disapproved of me. I hated that. And I felt that they were waiting tolerantly for me to give up my wild ideas and settle down to have children and be a nice young matron and occupy my days becomingly with contract bridge. I remarked to Cora that it was hopelessly banal of me to dislike my mother-in-law.

It gave me the feeling of living in the middle of a bad music-hall joke.

Well, we saw very little of them. Simon knew how I felt; he had grown away from them sufficiently to have very much the same feelings. We both loved his father, and one dinner a month could be borne. I said nothing, and reached for the cold cream.

Simon, gulping an aspirin, asked:

"Long or short coat, d'you know?"

"Long, I suppose. It's a dinner of eight, Gwen said."

"Are they going? Well, I hope to God that girl Katie hasn't sent my waistcoat buttons to the laundry again."

"No, I saw them. They're on your dressing-table."

"That's good."

He paused on his way to the door, and I saw his expression change. He came back and stood behind me, joining his hands together under the loose yellow wrapper that I was wearing.

"Do you love me?"

I felt tired and nervous. I had sat six hours at that desk, writing and re-writing exactly eight hundred words that remained cold, dead and unpliable as a block of wood. Everything seemed to crystallise suddenly to an irritating head. I said peevishly:

"Yes, of course I do."

"Not much, though."

"No, not much. I wish you'd let me move my arms. I want to go on dressing."

Simon said triumphantly, inevitably:

"You're in a damn bad temper this evening."

I felt quite incapable of replying. I wanted to say. "Leave me alone! I'm tired and miserable. I haven't done a stroke of good work for a month. I don't want to go and dine with your wretched family. You can all go to hell—to hell—to hell!" The words choked in my throat. I think that I had been working too hard. The greens and yellows of the room were suddenly unbearably irritating. I hated Simon's hands; the solidity of his neck and shoulders; the smile with which he was watching me. I wanted to be back in the little flat again, free to go to bed and sleep the bad temper out of my system.

Simon said quietly:

"Don't let's quarrel, my heart."

"Who's quarrelling? I wasn't quar—"

He sat down beside me on the long stool and drew me into his arms. All my nerves seemed to relax. I thought confusedly: "Yes, you'll always be able to get me that way, but intellectually I'm far stronger than you are—intellectually—I'm far. ..."

All that seemed so stupid, so unimportant. What did it matter who was weaker, who was stronger? It occurred to me that when we had first met we had circled round each other warily like prize-fighters looking for a weakness in the other's guard. From the beginning there had been a faint sense of antagonism between us; the antagonism of two intensely egotistical people, neither of whom enjoyed the sensation of giving in. We both had black, unforgiving tempers. When we were not being wildly, ecstatically happy we were quarrelling; there were no tame half-measures with us. The little house in Montpelier Place resembled a perpetual battle-ground; too often the truce was signed in this room, on that bed under the rather out-of-place plaque of a della Robbia Madonna and Bambino.

For a moment I felt insecure, as though I had walked on quicksand. I felt that something so wild, so intemperate and unequally balanced could not possibly last. The moment passed. Nothing seemed to matter but the fact that this was Simon, whom I adored.

"Oh, Simon darling, I'm sorry. I didn't mean to … I don't know … it's been such a beastly day."

"You've been depressed for weeks. What's the matter?"

I suggested, without much conviction:

"Perhaps I'm going to have a baby."

"My God, I hope not!" said Simon in an alarmed voice.

He was silent for a minute, busy with calculations.

"Well, I don't know how you could manage that."

"Oh, I don't know. One's even heard of cases of immaculate conception. I wish you'd go and turn on a bath, Simon."

But he lingered, playing with things on the dressing-table, opening boxes and looking inside them, sniffing the bottle of *Ce soir je t'aime* that he had given me for my birthday. Simon had a puzzling complex for liking women to use scent and have soft hands and wear silk things as sheer as petals. At least, it had puzzled me until I met Mrs. Quinn and found out the answer to lots of things about Simon.

"I'm sure you're working too hard at that damn writing of yours."

"Maybe."

"Worried about it?"

"No."

What was the use of saying "Yes?" I'd tried it before. It didn't work.

"On Saturday we'll go into the country and get two horses and ride. Or we'll buy some chocolate and go for a tramp on that bit of the Downs near Storrington. That's what you want, my girl."

"Darling, *will* you go and have a bath!"

He called out from his dressing-room:

"Chap at the office—awful nice chap—had just finished *Vulcan's Harvest*. He thought it was damn good."

"Oh, he did? Well, he's a liar. It's damn bad."

A copy lay on the side table; bright yellow paper jacket: *Vulcan's Harvest*, by Nevis Falconer, in modernistic black and silver lettering. I stared at it with dislike. It looked attractive enough, but it was a bad book. I was right. It was a damn bad book. I had stated the fact so brusquely to kill a small, lurking feeling of pleasure that someone had thought it good. I didn't want to fool myself that I hadn't produced a worthless, unsound bit of work. I was like those fanatics who get a dreadful sort of pleasure out of walking on knives with bare feet. Every time I thought of *Vulcan's Harvest* it was a separate stab, and I would deliberately try to prolong the pain.

It had come out in January, my first book since *The Forcing House*. I had started it just after we got married and moved into Montpelier Place. It was written in a preoccupied manner, as though I had snatched occasional five minutes from the business of adjusting myself to marriage and Simon and managing two not very expert servants. The stuff was smooth enough, but there was nothing of the bubbling well-spring of creation about it. This was just a shallow little stream that trickled neatly from the reservoir of other people's experience.

Now *The Forcing House* may have had some value, because it sprang directly from my own experience. I was not quite nineteen, and life in the forcing-house of a girls' school was still fresh in my head. The book wasn't a half-baked imitation of something else. I wrote it at white-heat in three months. *Vulcan's Harvest* took me nearly three years, and was the study of a middle-aged virgin living a life of repression in a narrow country town.

My God, what temerity! Looking back now, I can't think how I had the nerve to do it. I was twenty-one, and not even particularly interested in middle-aged people. I had never been repressed. I was not a virgin, and my experience of narrow country life consisted of living in Gloucestershire up to the age of six. Well, I got it into my head that *Vulcan's Harvest* was worth saving. For nearly three years I laboured over the body, and blew upon its cold flesh, and besought it to live. And lo! it was dead. It looked at me with glazed eyes. It drew not a single honest breath of life in all its 350 pages.

Ah, well! I dabbed the stopper of *Ce soir je t'aime* behind my ears and looked in the glass. Ugly, that bitter expression. Take it off, my girl, take it off. That's better. Simon came into the room, slim, in shirt-sleeves, fastening the strap of his white waistcoat. His hair lay sleek to his head, the waves brushed out; it shone a dusty reddish gold.

"What are you wearing? I don't like that black thing. Wear the white shiny one with no back."

By that he meant a beautiful white satin Lanvin that Kay Kirkpatrick, who played at being in a dress shop, had let me have cheap. Even then it had meant writing four loathsome articles and going without a new spring tailor-made. I protested feebly:

"But it seems such a waste, darling—only the family—"

But already I was opening the door of the built-in wardrobe, taking out the hanger. Simon said:

"I want to show you off to everyone. You're so lovely and so damn clever. I want everyone to say, 'Wonder why she married that Quinn chap?' … Hell's bells, Nevis, we're going to be late!"

III

I don't think that I was at all kind to the Quinns. In fact, I think that I was extremely unkind to them; the fact that I knew it did not make things any better. Really, with a little tolerance it was easy to understand why they did not consider me a suitable wife for Simon. But I had no tolerance at all. I was an intellectual snob and enjoyed being told that I was an intellectual snob. The disease can go no further.

Adrian Quinn, Simon's elder brother, had made the kind of marriage that pleased his father and mother—especially his mother. He had married Gwen Cunningham, who was one of the distinct type that I always thought of as Pont Street girls. That was because they seemed to flourish most profusely in Pont Street and the surrounding Cadogans. That was their native hunting-ground. In the mornings, at about half-past eleven, you would see them coming out with Sealyhams on jade-green leashes, or perhaps a couple of spotted Dalmatians. They all looked amazingly alike. Tall, slim, very pretty; little tricot caps from Agnès; silver fox scarves; Gunter's and the Berkeley. They gave lunches, at which their mothers did not appear, and bridge-teas; an astounding number of their afternoons were given up to bridge, which they played shrewdly, seriously, and well. They talked in high, clear voices and never said anything worth repeating, although they knew all the patter of the latest book and play.

They worked, too. They were for ever on some charity committee, getting up Silver Tulip Balls and Lucky Balls and Argentine Balls. They were very important and business-like about it ... and never once did they find out what it feels like to work so hard that one's eyes smart and one's brain collapses and one's body, ceasing to be a body, becomes just an aching, stupid lump of flesh. But often they were quite tired after a fast game of tennis or an extra hard canter in the Row. ... I wish I wasn't so bitter about people.

Well, from the Quinn point of view a Pont Street girl was the ideal wife, and Gwen Cunningham was perfectly typical. She had two nice babies, in a nice hygienic blue nursery with a cork floor and no pictures (they distract the budding mind— Modern Mothercraft), and a Nanny who was so crackly clean that she looked sterilised. Something else in Gwen's favour, you see. Mr. Cunningham was a banker—point Number Two. And when Mrs. Quinn rang up in the mornings she was not told that Mrs. Adrian was working and could not be disturbed.

I can sympathise a little with the Quinns now that a comfortable few thousand miles of ocean are stretched between them and me. For when one comes to think of it, their attitude was understandable. Adrian was the elder, the steadier son, but Simon was the favourite. Simon had the charm. And Simon produced suddenly, out of the blue, out of the chance encounter of a summer week-end at Burnham Beeches—Simon produced a young woman who lived by herself in a little flat with yellow walls and a geyser.

They could find nothing particularly wrong with my family except that I didn't live with them. They were even rather impressed by Granny, who was a mad, nasty-minded old woman, but had a tremendous dignity when they heaved her up out of bed and put on her false hair and all her bracelets. Mrs. Quinn was pleased, too, with the photographs of Falconer Court; it didn't matter that the place had been sold years ago, and that my grandmother and aunt lived in a funny little Victorian stucco cottage in the village.

What did matter was that I had exactly £200 a year of my own and what I made by writing. This last source of income was extremely problematical. And Mrs. Quinn viewed my writing with profound mistrust. She thought it "so clever" of me to write those little stories, but they weren't the sort she cared about; she read *The Forcing House* and found it "just a little coarse." Surely girls didn't really talk like that? After I married Simon she used to try and make me understand, gently and tactfully, that now I had become a Quinn there was really no need to work so hard.

"You look too thin, Nevis."

"Yes, I've been terribly busy with the new book."

"But, my dear, you don't have to do it now. You know that, don't you? I wish you'd eat more than you do and let your writing slip for the minute. You're looking much too thin and nervous. Well, if you insist, set aside a couple of hours a day for it."

And her eyes would openly, curiously search the lines of my figure which insisted on remaining unmaternally flat. Simon and I had talked over the children question and decided that we did not want to have any for a long time. We were both selfish. I was afraid that a child would interfere with my work, and Simon was afraid that it would interfere with my figure. Besides, there was no room in Montpelier Place. I knew what Simon would say if he had to struggle into his bath through a jungle of drying flannel diapers.

But in a way his mother was very like him. She was egotistical, but her egotism took the form of a rather ghoulish desire to see herself perpetuated; to live again through someone else's youth and vitality. She would have liked to harass and fuss me as she had harassed and fussed poor Gwen; to say, "Now leave it all to me, dear—you don't want worry at a time like this," and then drive everyone into a state of nervous frenzy before she had settled on specialist and nurse and the right make of baby-carriage. Luckily Gwen concealed the constitution of a cow under the exterior of a flower, and came through both confinements quite placidly. But my nerves were not so robust. I used to think that if ever we had a baby I should crawl away into a bush and have it peacefully by myself where Mrs. Quinn could not possibly get at me.

She had been a Miss Tracy-Yarborough of Leicestershire, and was considered to have taken a step down in marrying Edward Quinn, who was "in trade"—then almost a criminal offence. She was a hard, stupid woman. When I was first trying to understand Simon I used to be puzzled because he did not respond to teasing. If I teased him he turned surprised and stolid and dull; then, rather pathetically, he seemed to get the hang of it and would flush a quick, pleased red. I don't think any woman had ever teased him before. You could not picture Mrs. Quinn as a lovely, playful young mother. She said once that she had never used rouge or lipstick in her life. So Simon liked women to be soft and feminine and a bit exotic, to wear sheer silk things and put *Ce soir je t'aime* behind their ears.

My father-in-law was by far the best of the lot: a cheerful, rather common little man, with dapper shoulders and a depressed reddish moustache. In build and colouring he was something like Simon. I used to wonder how he had managed to build up the steel business in which Adrian was now a partner. He never struck me as being particularly intelligent, but he had managed to amass a considerable amount of money that one day, I suppose, would be divided between Adrian and Simon.

He was a kind and somehow rather pathetic creature. In moments of excitement an occasional aspirate came unstuck. At our wedding he said, "'Ow are you, Lady Falconer?" to my grandmother, who had been shipped down very carefully and painfully from Gloucestershire for the occasion, and my grandmother shouted in trumpet tones, "*Who* is that awful little man, Nevis?"

He and I made shy attempts at liking each other. I discovered that he was the only member of the Quinn family who read books, except Mrs. Quinn, who got Michael Arlen and Stephen McKenna from the Times Book Club. But old Edward read Tolstoi and de Quincy and Chesterton. He used to sneak me into his study to show me first editions that he had bought on the sly; it had to be concealed from Mrs. Quinn, who could not understand spending money on books when you could get such nice clean copies at the library.

His other weakness was his cellar, and we used to discuss fuders and years very solemnly. As a matter of fact, although I had picked up a bit from dining with middle-aged men at places like Boulestin's and the Eiffel Tower, I knew very little about it, but I had a good natural palate, and my father-in-law was immensely tickled to find a young woman whose ideas of wine extended beyond a syrupy Graves.

Adrian was like his mother in looks. He had the same long, thin body; the same arched nose; the same curiously light eyes that were the only characteristic that he shared with Simon. He knew a great deal about steel and horses, and nothing at all about art and literature, for which he had a profound contempt. He said, "I get through the *Times* every day, and that's about as much as I can do." As he failed in my intelligence tests (*a*), (*b*) and (*c*) (he would probably have guessed that Virginia Woolf was one of the runners for the Epsom Selling Plate), I thought him dull and extremely tedious. The elder of his two infants already showed signs of arching its nose, and the younger pointed knowingly at van horses in the street. Even in Adrian, you see, the Quinn egotism was a strong, ruthless force that left its mark on everything with which it came in contact. Poor little Gwen's children were not allowed to look like her; her individuality had been swamped by Adrian, as mine might have been swamped by Simon if I had not fought so hard.

Sometimes I would look at Simon and think, "How is it that you fascinate me as you do? How is it that you manage to combine the qualities of the man I adore and a Quinn? For really you are very like them. You are hard and obstinate and ruthless. You are stupid, but have a certain amount of shrewdness about money. You are intensely egotistical and maddeningly complacent about your ignorance of everything I love and respect. Altogether you represent a type that, normally speaking, I detest. We have nothing in common except sex. How is it that I ever thought we should make a success of marriage, and how is it that, barring five or six crashing rows a week, I seem to have thought right?"

Everything in my father-in-law's dining-room was large, ugly and expensive. The Victorian mustard-pots and pepper-castors, the solid silver candlesticks, even the peppermint sweets, seemed designed for a giant's table. My hands, of which I was rather proud, looked especially slender and childish as they grasped the massive knives and forks, (Tracy-Yarborough crest, an eagle with a ridiculous resemblance to Mrs. Quinn).

The curtains that shut out a double view of Prince's Gate were heavy tobacco-brown velvet, falling from a looped and braided pelmet. On the wall above the sideboard was a hideous and very valuable Dutch painting of six oysters in surprised conjunction with two dead pomegranates and a dead widgeon. Below it there was the subdued glitter of much silver, including some cups that Simon had won at Eton for running and high jump.

Except for Dr. and Mrs. Erskine it was an exclusively Quinn party. (I had still to remind myself that I was a Quinn, for I appeared in the telephone-book as Falconer, and usually signed myself that way.) But the Erskines were Quinns also, without their enormous vitality; prosperous middle-class people who drove a big Packard and sent their daughters to Court and went to the Italian Lakes for their holidays. He had an excellent practice in Harley Street, and always looked at me with a bluff, encouraging expression, as though to say: "Now, young woman, when are *you* going to have a baby?" His wife got her clothes from Jay's, and had the harassed, wispy look of one who is constantly woken up in the middle of the night by a peremptory telephone. You could picture her sitting up in bed, head in crimping-irons, and asking plaintively: "What is it, John dear? Another confinement or only a street accident?"

The conversation, as always, was almost exclusively family. My mother-in-law asked Gwen searching questions about Gwen's Nanny. Simon and Adrian talked horses across the table. Old Edward, his prominent eyes sliding furtively towards the low back of my Lanvin dress, murmured:

"Try that claret and tell me what you think of it. I've got

something new to show you after dinner, only mum's the word. Aldine Press—beautiful little bit of printing. Smart dress, that."

"Do you like it?"

"Oh, looks well on you. How's Simon doing in that cigarette business of his? Pity he won't come in with me. Nice wine, eh?"

The wine was good, the dinner excellent and stodgy. Before he married me Simon had eaten three meals like this every day and somehow survived. As I helped myself warily to chocolate soufflé, wreathed in cream, I reflected that an amusing treatise might be written on the importance of food in our lives. A Diet For Every Need. Inspiring breakfasts; witty luncheons, dinners to put passion into strong men. No one can commit adultery on a diet of salads and lightly-boiled eggs. Lives must have been ruined before now for want of a few underdone chump chops. ... My father-in-law asked me what I was laughing about.

But presently I disgraced myself in an argument on D. H. Lawrence. Mrs. Erskine had started it, rather unexpectedly. I think that she was by way of taking a timid interest in "art" in the intervals of going with the family to Como and packing the daughters and their feathers into Daimler Hires for a four hours' wait in the Mall. I remember saying that Lawrence was a sex reformer, and that we all ought to get back to the healthy Renaissance frankness of Boccaccio. I think that I wanted to see copies of *Lady Chatterley's Lover* distributed free to everyone over the age of fourteen. It was true that Lawrence was one of my gods, but I rather overdid things, conscious of a twinkle in old Edward's eye and an alarming rigidity at the other end of the table.

My mother-in-law, with the air of one retrieving a desperate situation and saving something from the wreck, said that Warwick Deeping wrote such nice stories.

I was in disgrace. The parlourmaid's pretty neck was pink

over her starched collar; the last quarter of an hour had been unusually entertaining. I noticed Simon looking at her neck, and was obscurely annoyed that it was a pretty one. I asked myself coldly: "Why not let things pass? Why must you always lose your temper and try to bait them? Oh, hell! That's what comes of an Irish mother, I suppose." I looked at Simon again, and saw that he was watching me with a funny little smile. Instantly everything was all right. I smiled back and thought: "Oh, I do love you. All these people are so stupid and unimportant. I ought to be strong-minded and not let them get on my nerves like this. I'll be extra nice to Mrs. Quinn when we go upstairs."

But Mrs. Quinn was coldly, reproachfully distant to me for the rest of the evening. I whispered to Edward: "I've put my foot in it again!"

He said: "Bless your 'eart, it's only one of Edith's moods. Let's slip off and I'll show you that Aldine. If you'd care for a spot of really good brandy, we'll have up the Napoleon. I only gave Erskine the second-best downstairs."

I sighed: "Edward darling, you're a great comfort."

He grunted and looked pleased.

"What did you pay for that rag you've got on? My word! Five pounds the square inch, eh? Well, it suits you. Send the bill along to me."

Two tables of bridge at a shilling a hundred. The ormolu clock struck eleven; there was a polite movement towards a tray of barley-water and decanters. Gwen, who had been playing at the other table, looked pale and tired. I managed to murmur:

"Well, my dear, how are things?"

"Don't say anything, but I'm going to have another baby in September."

"Oh, Gwen! It's *much* too soon after Timothy!"

"I know. As a matter of fact, it was an accident. Adrian's furious."

"Well, if it's not too late, why don't you do something about it?"

"Oh, I don't know." Gwen brought out an octagonal onyx case and rouged her lips without interest. Her lovely eyes were the bluest and emptiest I had ever seen. It seemed impossible that this brittle, immature creature should be a potential giver of life to three passionate, struggling and bewildered human animals. Snapping the case shut, she asked vaguely: "But isn't that rather a lot of trouble? I hate trouble. Anyway, for the Lord's sake, don't say anything to Mrs. Quinn yet."

"She'd be all over you, my dear. If she hasn't left you the family jewels already, she will now."

Gwen flushed and said:

"Don't be a fool. But it's such a beastly nuisance. There's Adrian black in the face, and I'd just got him to the point of agreeing to a month at Antibes this summer. Can you picture me lying about the rocks in a tight one-piece Jantzen?"

Mrs. Quinn bore down on us. Good-bye, good-bye, good-bye. Thanks so much; we have enjoyed it. Thank God that's over. Taxi! I lay back in my corner. Simon asked:

"Cigarette?"

"Please."

He was still smiling that funny little smile. The lid of his left eye was drooping, until it was almost closed. Looking sideways, I saw his profile against the dark lining of the cab: straight nose, good chin, that secretive smiling mouth.

"I do think you're rather beautiful, Simon. How did you ever get into that family?"

"You're damn hard on my family!"

"Well, they're pretty frightful."

"So are yours, for that matter."

He spoke a trifle peevishly. Usually he had a tremendous success with elderly ladies; they found his manner, interested and a shade deferential, quite charming. But my formidable grandmother had been unimpressed. When I took Simon up to Gloucestershire for a week-end to meet her, she greeted him with:

"So you're a short man. Can't abide short men. You'll be the first Falconer who's under six feet."

"But then, you see, I'm not a Falconer," said Simon, smiling amiably.

Granny took no notice. I don't think that she heard, or would have understood what he said. To her any man who was lucky enough to marry a Falconer woman became automatically a Falconer; in one or two cases the change of name had been actual. She placed a bull's-eye in her mouth and, still glaring at Simon, observed thickly:

"You'll be the runt of the family."

No, it hadn't been a success, that meeting.

"I know, darling, but it's a different kind of frightfulness. Old and dotty as Granny is, she wouldn't tolerate for a minute the sort of inane, deadly chit-chat that passes for conversation at Prince's Gate."

"You make too much fuss about conversation. It's all alike to me."

"No it isn't. It's either stimulating or dead. Dead as that awful widgeon in the dining-room!" I began to laugh. I laughed and laughed. "Oh, Simon, it's so funny, really! If only I didn't get cross!"

"You get on with the Governor all right, anyway."

"Yes, he's a pet. Why is it that men are so much nicer than women?"

"You like some women."

"Oh, Cora—and I'm quite fond of one or two in the way that I like seeing them now and then, and don't really care whether they're alive or dead. That's all. … What about going into the Berkeley for half-an-hour to show off the Lanvin?—Which, by the way, your divine parent is going to foot the bill for."

"All right."

He put his head out of the window to tell the driver. We turned back into the Brompton Road, past the silent block of Harrod's, where emaciated steel tubing ladies still displayed, rather pathetically, the latest things in sports clothes and lace brassieres. Hyde Park Corner; high-waisted grey overcoats clustering round the coffee-stall; St. George's Hospital; to remind one for a fleeting second that there is suffering within five minutes' brisk walk of where one dances to a saxophone. Piccadilly: tarts, prowling taxis, a cat shooting through the Park railings. To the right there is the darkness of trees and grass; much farther down, across the Mall, lights are reflected in the quiet water, and there is a warm, gummy smell of chestnut buds, and water-hens go "Peep!" But one is twenty-four; one must enjoy oneself; so one goes off to wedge one's tired body against other tired bodies, and say "Hallo!" to lots of silly people. *Ain't misbehavin', I'm savin' my love for you.* Oh, Lord! London, my London! The square white bulk of Devonshire House, and in a brilliantly-lit show-window a car as sleek, as taut, as frighteningly dark and powerful as the stripped torso of a prize-fighter. Simon leans forward.

"God, there's a car for you!"

"Yes, we might have one when the Bentley eventually falls to pieces. You get out first. Damn these long skirts!"

The familiar green walls and rose-pink curtains; the young

leader of the band crooning *Ain't misbehavin'*. I went into the cloak-room to leave my coat and spend a penny, to powder my already white nose and redden my already vermilion lips. I was pleased with the reflection of the Lanvin dress; pleased with the way my short dark hair grew in a crisp widow's peak off my forehead; pleased with the smallness of my breasts and the flatness of my behind. A Sealyham, dyspeptic with flattery and chicken sandwiches, was tied to the leg of the dressing-table. "Poor old duckums, then!" He looked at me with bulging eyes, yawned, flumped.

Simon was waiting outside; he was watching, with that curious knack of becoming suddenly absorbed in something, the sliding scurry of waiters through the service-door. Simon in tails always looked particularly fair, clean-cut and dangerous; a bit of a dandy with a dark carnation in the lapel of his coat. The band had changed its tune. It was playing *Don't Ever Leave Me!* I hummed it softly, and was suddenly glad that I was twenty-four and wearing a beautiful dress, and that there were times when it was nice to be just silly, just young. I forgot that three hours ago I had been bored and miserable; that six hours ago I had been hunched up over a desk, trying to galvanise eight hundred listless, clammy words into life. I forgot my ambition to write a good book; to study, to work, to march unflinchingly towards that single aim. I forgot the nightmare that had a way lately of cropping up between thinking and not thinking: the grisly little nightmare that never again would I be able to write anything so good as *The Forcing House*.

I said to Simon:

"Let's dance."

"All right. It's packed, but Ferraro says he'll find us a table somewhere."

No one ever danced so well as Simon. He could not help it; he had the right sort of body. He was the most perfect mover I have ever seen. And it was funny that he could not sing a tune to save his life, yet had such a gorgeous sense of rhythm. The thought came into my head: What a pity we can't always be dancing—then we wouldn't quarrel. I laughed. Simon's arm tightened round my body.

"What's the joke?"

"I love you. It's so damn funny."

"Got anything on under this frock?"

"Not much."

"Thought so. You'll be had up!"

The room was very full. We saw plenty of people we knew; young couples like ourselves who were always complaining that they were hard up, ruined, had hard-hearted bank-managers, and yet always managed to dance at the Berkeley and race at Sandown and drive a fast sports car. We spent up to the last penny of next year's income, yet it never occurred to us that we might give up going to all the usual places and doing the usual things. I said so to Simon as we sat drinking beer and eating the last of the oysters. He said:

"God knows why. This sort of thing is pretty damsilly, really."

"Ye-es, I suppose so. I don't know. I enjoy it."

"You ought to have been a miner's wife and had fourteen children. Then you'd have written something worth reading."

I didn't answer. Some vague idea for a new book had come into my head out of the blue, out of the froth on my tall glass of lager. That is the way things get started with me. A white orchid in a shop-window; a woman rushing out of a house, frantically putting on black kid gloves; someone says as they pass me in the street, "What was I to do? I couldn't very well ask her—"

a torn newspaper gambols dustily across the road. Any one of those things is enough to start that whirling feeling in the head, that sense of lightness and power which will suddenly reveal who is going to buy the white orchid and take it home; who threw down the newspaper after one panic-stricken glance; why the woman with the black kid gloves is rushing down the steps and into the waiting taxi. ...

Yes, I would write about the things and the places I knew. I would write about Simon, Gwen and Adrian, Cora, Roddy Talent ... Why not? At least I knew my stuff. I had that pull over the old hands. And now that I come to think of it, I've got a lot to say. Why not? I began to feel excited and fierce and happy, riding on top of the world. First chapters get themselves written in moods like that, and one is always fond of them, as one is fond of children who are born from moments of love.

I looked across at Simon to tell him, and—didn't tell him. I had learnt better by now. Simon would listen and say heartily: "That sounds all right to me," and the marvellous moment would have gone. The bloom would be off the leaf; the flower would have fallen. What did I want? I wanted someone who would lean forward and say ...

Simon said:

"What about having one more turn and then going? It's hot as hell in here."

"All right."

Montpelier Place was very quiet. It had the look of space and clarity that streets have by lamp-light at one o'clock in the morning. One of the houses had eighteen-century wrought-iron brackets to hold torches. I thought of the days when the dew rose off the market-gardens of Knightsbridge, of Smollett noticing the rich look of the crops in Kensington. Crash! Two cats, a black and a tabby, bounded out of an area and streaked up the road. I sighed.

"Better have an old boot handy to-night," said Simon.

The yellow walls of the little hall looked attractive as we went in and bolted the door. There were no letters, but on the telephone-messages pad Katie had written: "Mr. Marcus Chard rang up Mrs. Quinn and will ring again to-morrow morning." Simon looked over my shoulder.

"Who's he?"

"Lord knows."

But I still stood there frowning at the pad. The name sounded vaguely familiar. Marcus Chard. I had the feeling that I had seen it somewhere engraved in the left-hand corner of impressive man-sized stationery. Well, it didn't really matter. Whoever he was, Mr. Chard would ring up to-morrow.

Simon came out of the living-room as I started upstairs. He said:

"There are some dead flowers in there. Tell Katie to change them. You're slack as hell."

I murmured without rancour:

"Oh, go to hell."

IV

🐾

The breakfast table-cloth was parrot-green and yellow in broad stripes on coarse linen, very gay, someone had brought me half a dozen from St. Jean-de-Luz. My dressing-gown was green, too, cut exactly like a man's. In spite of Simon's objections I could not get out of the habit of coming down to coffee and grape-fruit in a dressing-gown. But Simon liked women to be crisp and corseted behind the coffee-pot, at a quarter to nine. In some mysterious way they had to combine this with soft femininity, trailing chiffons, and *Ce soir je t'aime* at five pounds a bottle.

He came back to say:

"I've left out a suit on the bed in my dressing-room. You might take it round to the cleaner's for me."

"All right."

"Don't forget to tell Katie about those flowers."

"All right."

"Good-bye, darling."

"'Bye."

The front door slammed. Another day had begun. I helped myself to honey, read Mr. Hannen Swaffer without interest, and remembered that I had forgotten to ask Simon two or three quite important things.

It was another wonderful day. As I fastened the cuff of my grey and red jersey dress, I had a sudden temptation to chuck work; to get the car and go and see how spring was making headway in the woods and hedges. Burnham Beeches, perhaps. But no, I had an absurd nostalgia for pine trees; for steep banks starred with watery yellow primroses and the glossy blue and green of periwinkles; for a little Norman church with faded frescoes and a dusty harmonium. Hilda could make me up some sandwiches. ... Well, it just couldn't be done, that's all. Work, my dear; work is the lot of the young and ambitious.

The telephone-bell rang. There was an extension by my bed. I took off the receiver.

"'Lo."

"Mrs. Quinn? Savoy Hotel—Mr. Chard calling. One minute, please." My brain began to work very quickly. Savoy Hotel. Americans stay Savoy Hotel, Chard was an American. Yes, half a minute. I'd nearly got it that time. Chard was something to do. ...

"Hallo! Mrs. Quinn? This is Marcus Chard here."

"Oh, yes, of course." Nice voice, but who the hell are you, anyway?

"I don't believe we've ever had the pleasure of corresponding. Mr. Stancy usually handles your books, but—"

"Why, of course!"

Crocker & Stancy, West 42nd Street, New York. In a flash of photographic clarity I saw their thick impressive notepaper; the three names engraved in black in the top left-hand corner:

> Harvey B. Crocker.
> William Platt Stancy.
> Marcus Chard.

"I'd like so much to meet you while I'm over here, Mrs. Quinn—or do you still keep to Miss Falconer?"

"Whenever possible!"

"Well, now, Miss Nevis Falconer, when can we meet?"

"How long are you staying here?"

"Not more than a couple of weeks. Then I'm planning to go to Russia. Can you come down here and lunch with me to-day?"

"I don't lunch out on week-days as a rule."

"You're quite right. It's the only way to get work done. But when it's the case of a business talk. ... You will? That's fine! I'll be waiting in the little lobby outside the grill-room, one o'clock."

"How am I going to recognise you?"

"You won't. But I'll know you from those photographs you sent over for the publicity department. *Vulcan's Harvest* is in our late spring list, you know. ... Well, we'll talk about all that at lunch."

"Yes. One o'clock. Good-bye, Mr. Chard."

I was not conscious of any great feelings of enthusiasm. These business talks with editors and publishers always seemed to turn out the same way: they had you down to their office or their suite at the Savoy; they were heavily paternal; they explained exactly how they wanted you to write an article or a story for them. And then you went quietly home and wrote it quite differently. And usually they took it. Which was pleasant, but rather a waste of everyone's time.

Still, it would mean one less meal to be ordered to-day. I went down to see Hilda, who was standing in the sunlight at the back door, chatting to the baker's boy.

I did not like ordering meals. I did not like managing servants, because I persisted in regarding them as human beings, and the result was that they thought I was a complete fool. Simon, who treated them as though they were mechanical Robots with two pairs of hands apiece, got excellent service and dog-like devotion. He had only to go to the top of the kitchen stairs and shout down: "Where are my boot-jacks? Why isn't there any beer in the sideboard cupboard?" and Katie and Hilda fell over each other.

In three years we had sampled every kind. There was Vi'let, whose invariable answer when I asked her to suggest a sweet for dinner was: "Aow! Whatabout a narse milk pudding?" There was Grace, with the face of a Fra Lippo Lippi angel and the unfortunate *penchant* for having young men in her bedroom when we went away for week-ends. (It seemed to me very natural, but Mrs. Quinn descended on Montpelier Place, all nose and no lips, and insisted that she should be sacked.) We had even tried a married couple who were very willing, and broke everything and sent up oysters without their shells, naked and clammy, on a paper d'oyley.

I hated going to all the shops and choosing the food. In our flat-dwelling days Mother had always looked after that; then I had depended on Proutie and the little restaurant round the corner. I had never had to go and pinch dead chickens in rude places to find out whether they were young or not; to mark if the turbot's eye met mine candidly, or with the glazed heaviness of a fishy hang-over. But I tried to be immensely knowledgeable about it all. Everyone in the shop would seem very much amused and I would back nervously into rows of boiling-fowls, feeling young and confused and horribly conscious that the presiding girl at the cash-desk was listening with a tolerant smile. After which they would send me bad fish, and meat that was all bone and fat. Damn!

Luckily Hilda had taken all that off my hands, and sallied out every morning with a large string bag. She was a stocky, fresh-coloured girl with glasses, a "young man" who came and sat speechlessly in the kitchen on Sunday afternoons, and no imagination. Now I had plenty of imagination. I knew, in theory, a good deal about food; I knew how it ought to be, and when anything went wrong it irritated me to death. It was the same with the house. I was fond of the house; I knew how it ought to look. Spotless paint, polished walnut, lots of fresh flowers. But Katie seemed to have a religion that forbade her to dust in corners, and I was always busy, and … my God, I must remember to tell her about those dead daffodils!

Hilda had to be handled so tactfully, too. It was no use giving her one of Marcel Boulestin's recipes out of *Vogue* and saying "Try that next time we're alone." She was frightened to death at the mention of half-a-pint of Béchamel sauce and six cooking oysters and a glass of old brandy. So our morning conferences were generally as uninspired as this:

"Good-morning, Hilda."

"Good-morning, m'm."

"We're in to-night, Hilda. What about a nice soufflé of fish?"

"That would be nice, m'm."

"And cutlets—no, we had cutlets on Wednesday." Why is it that I can never think of any animal but a sheep and any part of the sheep but cutlets? "We might have little fillets of beef and mushrooms, and—what sort of sweet, d'you think, Hilda?"

"What would be nice, m'm?"

You damn fool, that's what I'm asking you! I look up at the kitchen ceiling for inspiration. None comes. "Make it a savoury. I don't know what kind."

Look of panic behind Hilda's glasses. She is the kind of fool who wants everything written down in black-and-white. What does she really think of me, I wonder?

"A Welsh rarebit, Hilda."

"Yes, m'm. What about lunch, m'm?"

"I'm out. Tell the greengrocer that last lot of grape-fruit was frightful. And Mr. Quinn has been asking for fried plaice for breakfast."

There! Pouf! Over for the day! I escape, humming the tunes of the night before and feeling about ten years old. When I've written a best seller we'll live in a service flat. Two clear hours, anyway, until I need change for my lunch with Mr. Chard. I shut the door, sit down at the desk, bring out a wad of papers. Two clear ...

I spring up, rush to the door, and call out, "Katie!" No answer. The girl is deaf. Sounds of loud, cheerful singing float down from the bathroom.

"Katie! Kat-eee!"

Silence. A head pops over the bannisters.

"Did you call, m'm?"

"Yes, I did. Several times. There are some dead flowers in here, Katie. Come and take them out."

"Yes, m'm."

She sounds injured and resentful. I sit down again, but the first mood of optimism has gone. I read over what I wrote yesterday. Yes, it's bad, loosely constructed, dead. ... Why can't that girl take the flowers out when she sees they're dead? Hilda is really the better-tempered of the two ... Simon doesn't like cheese savouries. Hell!

What an irritating noise a carpet-sweeper makes! It seems to go backwards and forwards interminably, squeaking and whining, cutting through my thoughts. Now there's a lull. She must be answering the telephone. Yes, she's coming downstairs.

"Please, m'm, Mrs. Kirkpatrick is sorry to worry you, but can she speak to you for a minute on the 'phone?"

"Katie, how many times have I told you that I'm not to be disturbed when I'm working? Next time I shall be really angry. Ask Mrs. Kirkpatrick to leave a message."

"Yes, m'm."

Oh, lord! another domestic crisis brewing, but peace for a couple of hours, at any rate. What can Kay have wanted, I wonder? Forget it! I drew the pad of paper towards me, and wrote:

"Up to then it had always been easy to keep personalities out of her work, not only because there was no time, but because of those seventeen years that had turned her into an impersonal little machine with two lynx eyes and a pair of unerring scissors,"—I wonder if Kay wanted to find out about that party at the Café Anglais on Tuesday. ... "Miss Clothilde could look at a beautiful body with as much emotion as a factory hand looks at a bottle on which he is about to stick a label. ..."

Katie at the door again.

"Please, m'm, I'm sorry to worry you, but it's Mr. Quinn on the 'phone, and you know you said always to tell you when he rings up."

"All right. I'll go."

Lord, why isn't there some island where all the writers in the world can retire together, and work and sulk and never answer telephones?

"'Lo, Simon?"

"That you, Nevis? Listen, darling, I believe I've put out the wrong suit to be sent to the cleaners'. I think I put out the dark-blue with the very faint red line. Well, it's the other dark-blue—the older one."

"All right."

"You sound a bit blue. What's wrong?"

"Every damn thing."

"If you don't cheer up I'll begin to think that what we said last night is really coming true."

"What's that?"

"Baby."

"Don't be a damn fool," I said crossly.

I heard Simon laugh.

"All right. I'll be home early. Don't forget about the suit. 'Bye, darling."

I went back to the living-room and lit a cigarette and stared blindly at myself in the little Venetian glass. I thought: "This is what you've let yourself in for. Nevis Falconer or Mrs. Simon Quinn, which is it to be? Why don't you make up your mind to stop fighting altogether, or else cut and run?"

The cigarette ash grew long and burnt my fingers. I hurled it into the grate and sobbed out suddenly: "Oh, to hell with everyone!" and dropped in a miserable heap on the cushions under Cora's Flemish flower-picture. Cora, the only person in the world who might possibly have understood, and she was down at Burnham being a good wife to that self-satisfied ass, Frank Fenton. The whole world was against me. I hated Simon. I loved him helplessly. I wanted to think: "Go away! Go to hell! You're spoiling my work. You're taking away from me the only thing I really love." I thought: "The dark-blue suit—not the one with the faint red line. If I say express, they'll have it done by Monday or Tuesday. ..."

The little lobby outside the Savoy Grill, one o'clock. Everyone was there. That is to say, there were present at least half-a-dozen people whose faces would have been familiar to the readers of illustrated papers and totally meaningless to countless millions. But it is a habit to say that everyone was there, as though one's own particular little lot were the whole sea instead of an insignificant little patch of pebbles on one particular beach. Simon used to say that I suffered from the disease rather badly.

I had dressed quite carefully for my lunch with Marcus Chard. The dark-green tailor-made was sophisticated, but the crisp ruffled blouse gave an air of youthfulness—very important, this. "Well, I knew you were a kid when you wrote *The Forcing House*, but I never thought ..." I had a weakness for tiny tricot turbans; I thought that they made my face look haggard and interesting, and, being twenty-four, I longed to be thought haggard and interesting. But lunch with Mr. Chard seemed to call for something else. I chose the little dark-green felt with the brim cut well off the forehead. Green turns my grey eyes quite yellow. A gardenia from Solomon's in my buttonhole, black kid pumps, black kid Lafarge bag. In the taxi going down to the Savoy I put on a touch more lipstick. ... Heigh-ho! The man will certainly look at me and say: "Did we say 12½% royalties, Miss Falconer? It was a mistake, Miss Falconer. I think I am at liberty to promise 20%, Miss Falconer, if you will kindly step upstairs to my suite for a few minutes." Nice to be an idiot occasionally.

But where was Mr. Chard? The lobby was full of men. Men in grey suits and brown suits and black suits. Some of them stared at me, but only with the impersonal interest of males in a (solitary and moderately attractive) female. I sat down. And suddenly a man detached himself from the group round the entrance to the Men's cloak-room. English tailoring but definitely American round the neck. What is it? Is it the collar, the shirt? Is it merely the neck? Is it … I thought to myself: "*Voilà* Mr. Chard!"

"It is Miss Falconer, isn't it?"

"Yes."

"I'm very glad to meet you at last. Sit down and we'll have cocktails. Or would you rather have them inside?"

"No, let's have them here."

"Fine. What sort do you like? Sidecar? Two Sidecars, please. Can you smoke these American things? I brought over a lot with me."

"Yes, I like them."

He had rather remarkable hands. I had just been reading *Jew Suss* for the second time, and I remembered the description of Karl Alexander's hands: "slim, bony and hairy on the back, but fleshy, fat and short on the palm." Mr. Chard's hands were like that; the fingers were long and muscular, but the palms were thick and looked soft. Dark hair grew down from the wrists. They were beautifully manicured and wore two signet rings.

I looked up and said:

"So you recognised me all right."

"Yes, indeed." He laughed. "To be frank, I spotted you when you came in, but I waited a couple of minutes and took a good look. Those photographs you sent over aren't complimentary."

"Well, they were expensive enough!" It's the hat—I told you so.

"They're very lovely but they make you look hard. I was prepared for someone a good deal older-looking and a bit sophisticated and hard-boiled."

Why, you fool, I *am* hard! Hard as nails. I fight like blazes to be hard. It must be this hat and the ruffled blouse that's giving me a sweet, ingenuous, virginal expression. The boy in the white linen coat brought our Sidecars. I leant back and studied Mr. Chard.

Marcus Chard must have been somewhere in the early forties. He was about Simon's height, but much broader; enormous shoulders and a thick bull neck. In another few years he would be definitely stout. He had a broad, flattish face; a good nose with flaring nostrils; a heavy dark jaw shaved so closely that it looked glossy. His thick dark hair was brushed back from a square forehead. I did not altogether care for the expression of his eyes. They were too unpleasantly acute; too small; too shrewd and brown and lively. But when he smiled their whole expression changed. They almost disappeared in fan-shaped wrinkles of laughter; his face became good-natured and benevolent. He had, too, very beautiful teeth, white, strong and even.

We went in to lunch. The waiters were very attentive to him. We were put at a table where we could see and be seen. He ordered lunch, swiftly, deliberately, not consulting me at all. I rather liked that. We talked of crossings, the newly-built *Europa*; of bull-terriers, changing London, "Journey's End," the Theatre Guild. He talked extremely well. He had an amusing mind and a funny, original turn of speech; he seemed to have read everything and been everywhere and known everybody. I began to enjoy my lunch. I had a feeling that he liked me. At last he said:

"And now about you."

"Yes." My heart sank. "And now about *Vulcan's Harvest*." Marcus Chard was the sort of person who would tell the truth, and tell it trenchantly, bitingly. Already he had said hard things about several people and their writing.

"Do you know, I'm very interested in you? You were one of the first people I called up when I got in yesterday."

"That's nice of you."

"Not really. Just curiosity. As I said over the 'phone, this morning, I've never handled your books. When you first came to us Stancy took care of you. You've met Stancy."

"Yes, about three years ago."

"He came back and made me curious about you. I was interested in your stuff already. *The Forcing House* was a grand piece of work—we were proud to have it on our list."

He paused and looked at me. His face was kind. His eyes were quick and darting and sympathetic.

"Cigarette?"

"No, thanks."

"Do you mind if I …?"

"Please go ahead."

"It's a pernicious habit between courses. … Well! Now listen to me, Miss Nevis Falconer. Just what has happened to you lately?"

"I …"

"No, listen. I'll tell you. I'll tell you frankly. And please don't mind if I step rather heavily on your feelings. I'm going to start off by saying I've got a hunch you're going to do something. As yet I don't know what—*The Forcing House* didn't really give much indication as to how the wind was blowing—but it's going to be something big. Do you feel that?"

"Yes."

He gave a roar of laughter.

"Great! That's great! Well, I don't mind telling you that three years ago I wouldn't have had a bit of hesitation in naming you as the best bet among the younger writers. That's the truth I'm a brusque, uncomplimentary person—"

"But you'd hesitate now."

He said deliberately, his eyes on my face:

"Yes, I'd hesitate now."

I felt the queerest mixture of anger and misery and relief. It was the kind of feeling you might have if you said to a doctor: "Tell me the worst," and he answered: "Six months to live." It was as though, after a lot of evasive probing round a mortal wound, one swift thrust had laid it bare. A wrench of supreme pain and then a queer sort of peace. Now I know the worst. Now nothing can hurt me any more. It was what I had been wanting all the time, subconsciously. Someone with guts enough to say "You're a flop, and you know it." Not Simon coming back from the office with his tales of awful nice chaps who had thought *Vulcan's Harvest* damn good. I didn't want a comforting salve of lies and good-nature. I wanted a hard, surgical *slash-slash*; an incisive cutting agony that would either cure or kill. Only that morning I had been sobbing angrily under the Flemish flower picture for want of someone like Marcus Chard.

He said slowly:

"I'm puzzled. I don't mind admitting it. When Stancy passed on *Vulcan's Harvest* to me in manuscript I kept on going back to the title-page to see if you really had written it. It's not a bad book. Don't think that. It's well written—technically you've advanced. But—"

"I know. You needn't tell me. Dead—not a kick to it."

"Now you're looking like those photographs. Please take off that expression." His face was so comically distressed and beseeching that I had to laugh.

"It's my natural expression, really."

"Don't try and kid yourself. I don't believe you, anyway. How's the asparagus?"

"Very good."

"Listen, my dear child. When I said just now that I'd hesitate, I didn't mean that I've lost faith in you. I haven't. You're naturally too good a writer to go out like a candle. But I'm wondering what exactly was the reason for *Vulcan's Harvest*."

"I got married."

"I see. Yes. You got married," said Mr. Chard slowly.

There was a pause. He seemed absorbed in twisting the onyx signet ring round and round his little finger. Extraordinary, those hands with their soft pink palms and the darkness of hair along their backs. I watched them, fascinated. He had rather long arms for the length of his body. There was something a little ape-like. ... He glanced up quickly, smiling.

"Well, we're bringing it out next month. I think it will make a good show. We've got out a stunning jacket for it—did the London office forward you on the first proofs? They did? And you liked it?"

We talked idly, impersonally, until I said that I must go, and began to gather up bag and gloves. Then he looked at me with a queer expression.

"I wonder what you're really thinking of me."

"Thinking of you?"

"Not angry at all?"

"Angry! I'm grateful! It's put me in a fighting spirit. I feel like going home and writing a masterpiece and sending the whole world to blazes."

"Great! That's absolutely the spirit. And one day you will— I'm certain of that."

We got up to go. I caught sight of myself in a glass, flushed, bright-eyed. For the first time in months I had the feeling that I wanted to sit down and work. I wanted to write until my muscles screamed and my head buzzed and the pen fell out of my hand. It was as though a numbing frost had broken, and the brooks were flowing again, the live torrents were gushing. I felt so grateful to Marcus Chard that I held out both my hands towards him and said:

"We must meet again before you go. When does the Russia trip come off, by the way?"

He looked down at my hands, held in both his own. He looked up again, without meeting my eyes. ... What's he looking at my mouth for? Have I got on too much lipstick?

"I don't know. It's rather uncertain. I may not go at all."

"Oh, that's too bad!"

"I don't know. I'm very fond of England. Do you know this is the first time I've been over for six years? And I'm going to stay over—in Europe, anyway—for quite a while."

"You must meet Simon before you go to Russia." As I spoke I had an instant conviction that they would hate each other, but it couldn't be helped.

"Is that your husband? I'd be glad to. And perhaps you'll come and dine with me one night, do a theatre?"

"That would be nice."

"Very well. I'll call you up in a day or two. *Au revoir.*"

He took me outside and put me into a taxi. The courtyard was full of sunshine. Two porters were shifting a group of wardrobe trunks, very smart tan and grey ones stuck over with bright labels: "Hôtel Royal, Danieli, Venezia," "Palace, St. Moritz." Two American women passed, chattering shrilly, their slim ankles twinkling in fish-net stockings, their foreheads startlingly naked under twin Agnès berets pushed well to the back of the head. "I thought it would look kind of mean in just the plain satin without the fox. ..." Off to spend more money. Pleasant occupation on a day like this. Opposite, in the little flower-shop, a writhing coil of striped and speckled orchids. They remind me of cobras with their queer marking, their narrow, wicked heads; graceful and deadly and obscene; prisoners behind glass until the American lady with the naked forehead buys them to pin on satin-not-so-plain. ...

My taxi was caught in a block at the entrance to the courtyard. I glanced out of the little window at the back, and there was Marcus Chard's thick, compact figure, still standing where I had left him. His hands were in his pockets, his head was thrown back. He was quite immobile, lost in thought. Suddenly he seemed to shake himself and walked quickly into the Court. My taxi lurched forward. I thought: "Funny man. Nice. I like him. Rather fascinating, in a way. ... Simon will be pretty insulting to him, probably. He hates all my friends before he's even seen them."

I let myself into the house. The afternoon post had just come. There was a thin brown packet; one or two belated press notices of *Vulcan's Harvest*. I always said, "Of course I don't give a damn about press notices—they don't mean a thing"—and then read them all and was cast down into the mire for weeks by a bad one. "This ably constructed novel shows considerable insight into the springs of action"—now what the devil does that mean? "Miss Falconer writes with such obvious sincerity and, occasionally, such real power and beauty that it is a pity her theme is not worth ...." Oh, to hell! When I retreat to my island there won't be any book reviewers there, either.

I ran upstairs, pulling off my hat. I almost fell down at the writing-table and drew a pad of paper towards me. It seemed only about twenty minutes later that Simon came into the room. I looked at him in a dazed way.

"Hallo, aren't you early?"

"No, I'm late. It's nearly half-past seven. I had to stay on. My God, if the bath-water isn't hot there's going to be the hell of a row."

I felt stupid and sleepy and contented. I put down my pen and stretched with sensuous enjoyment. There is nothing in the world to equal the satisfaction of working well, and then lying back and thinking "There!" Simon was looking at the gardenia.

"You're pretty smart."

"I've been out to lunch."

"Who with?"

"Marcus Chard."

"Who the hell's Marcus Chard?"

I told him. His eyelids drooped.

"Oh, God! An American."

He was one of those people who are convinced that all Americans have loud, twanging voices and are vulgar, incomprehensible barbarians who exist solely for the purpose of being sponged upon by stout-hearted Englishmen. He had known perhaps three in his life. It delighted him to hear of anyone going to America and making money there. He was stubborn and prejudiced about it as he was stubborn and prejudiced about books and music and painting my nails red and young men who had lilies in their rooms and went every night to the Russian Ballet. I would rage at him: "You're pig-headed and intolerant and stupid! You shut out of your life everything that you don't understand and one day you're going to miss something!" He would smile and say in his most blandly irritating voice: "You're right. I'm pig-headed and intolerant and stupid. Come and kiss me. I love you when you get angry and sparks fly out of your funny grey eyes." I would wail helplessly: "Oh, what's the use? ..." What was the use? I said:

"Yes, an American. Rather a charming one."

"Glad you enjoyed yourself. I've been thinking, Nevis. We ought to get a dog. What about it?"

"If you feed it and wash it and brush it, and teach it to use the garden instead of my bedroom carpet."

"My God, I've never known such a little slacker! Here you are, with nothing to do all day—"

"Yes, darling, here I am all day with nothing to do except work myself stupid. Don't be such a damn fool."

He went upstairs; I heard him shouting "Katie." Neither of us had inquired about each other's work for the simple reason that we didn't give a damn. I stood by the window for some minutes, staring rather vaguely into the street. Much the same as last evening—lettuce-green front door opposite, a Bentley waiting outside, hawker coming round the corner with a basket of pale lavender tulips. But things seemed different to-night. I felt tired but happy. I kept on thinking of Marcus Chard's voice and his clever, darting eyes as he said: "It's going to be something big. Do you feel that?"

V

Occasionally Simon and I gave uneasy dinner-parties to our friends. They were uneasy because no kind of a party can be a success unless there is some subtle inner concord between host and hostess. Without that the hospitable atmosphere wilts, the evening goes to pieces. It made me mad because I remembered the gay little parties I used to give at the flat—never enough forks to go round, cold stuff from Fortnum's, and Proutie in her best plum-coloured velveteen, breathing loudly as she handed the vegetables. But, my Lord, those evenings had gone with a bang! They sparkled; people enjoyed coming to them and sitting on bedroom chairs and drinking sherry out of odd Woolworth glasses. The parties that Simon and I gave died dismally on their feet, no matter how attractive my green room looked with flowers, or how masterly a cheese soufflé poor Hilda sent upstairs. The food and the setting were all right; it was the host and hostess who were all wrong.

Simon could not stand my friends. When they came to dinner he was either blandly stupid or wilfully insulting. If the conversation turned on books he would say, "Don't know—never read a thing. Practically illiterate, aren't I, Nevis?" He would listen to their stories with a hard stare, and then begin to talk loudly about horses. He was usually so infuriating that I would be too crushed to make any efforts to pull the disconcerted party together again.

Simon's friends were divided into two categories—people he invited for business reasons and people he really liked. The business friends referred to me as "your good lady" and talked Mellow Cigarettes all through dinner, while their wives made stupid ineffectual remarks about servants and the new length of skirts. After dinner Simon would stay an interminable time drinking port. As I sat with the wife, half my mind would be listening for a stir from the little dining-room, the other half intent on not turning too glassy a smile to the profundities of "… don't really care for Gladys Cooper … godets in the skirt … men in the kitchen …." Quaite, quaite, quaite! I suffered—honestly and acutely suffered—at those dinners.

The people he liked were not much better. They were Good Chaps. They were Nature's Girl Guides and Boy Scouts. They discussed in loud, robust voices the sort of things that Simon enjoyed discussing; for the most part they were young and presentable, and they filled my soul with unspeakable boredom. Usually they would try to be kind and ignore the fact that I wrote books, or else they would make rather awful little jokes about it, and Simon would laugh loudly. It appalled me to see him sitting at ease among them, eyelids drooping, body lax and content, while my own was rigid with the effort of concentration necessary to stop myself from smashing something and rushing out of the house.

My friends were nearly all men, which made things a bit difficult. I did not like women, taken as a sex. I had tried, but their chatter about servants and babies and insides nearly drove me crazy. I saw all my own meannesses of soul reflected in them; the streaks of pretty femininity that would always make my writing lack the vigour, the clarity and impersonal detachment of a man's writing. I had been brought up with boy-cousins; in the holidays I used to be tearing over the countryside with them like a pack of wild ponies, instead of yearning with other girls in corners about sex. It was natural for me to get along better with men, and I did not see why I should be expected to drop all these friendships directly I married Simon.

He thought differently. His whole trouble was that he had been born three thousand years too late. That was at once his charm and his danger. His whole philosophy of life was as simple and direct as that of a man squatting on his bare heels and rubbing two stones together to make fire. Simon knew what he wanted and took it. At the beginning that crudeness and directness had fascinated me; it still fascinated me, but I fought against it. I knew that intellectually I could beat him; the knowledge seemed as stupid and ineffectual as though I had tried to wave a rapier in the face of some ruthless natural force like an earthquake or an avalanche. Ordinary rules did not apply to Simon because he ignored them all. It was no use reminding myself that I knew all about the Carolinan poets when I was being overridden by someone who did not know a Carolinan poet from Goddamn, and cared less.

We quarrelled continually. We were quarrelling on the day after my first lunch with Marcus Chard. Roddy Talent was giving a party that evening; up till then I had not been really keen to go, but now that Simon was opposing it I felt certain that it would be amusing. Besides, I had spent the morning having a shampoo, cut and manicure. It seemed a pity to waste it just going quietly to bed.

"I suppose it's no use trying to make you go?"

"I'm not particularly keen on your Nance friends."

"Oh, you're perfectly insufferable!"

"Maybe," he said complacently.

I looked at him in helpless, speechless fury. Sometimes I hated him for having the power to make me lose control so completely; to make me forget that I was a fastidious, civilised individual with a sense of humour and a tolerable amount of intelligence, and make me conscious only of a poor, bewildered body that blundered between rage and jealousy and desire. I hated his reddish foxy look and his hard, dry lips. I would find myself listening with a sensation of horror to the sound of my own voice. Naturally it was deep and soft. In these quarrels with Simon it rose to the querulous, unlovely note that we heard so often when the public-house at the corner closed on Saturday nights. The man would walk a little ahead; the woman would follow three paces behind, her mean shoulders bowed, her voice shrill and defiant. Those women with their awful hands and their soggy, anxious faces. ...

I looked down at my own hands with a sensation of relief—so slim, so pretty, the nails rosy and shining. That seemed to cool me, somehow.

"Well, for God's sake don't let's quarrel. It's too tiring."

"I wasn't quarrelling."

That was the maddening part, because it happened to be true. Simon rarely lost his temper outwardly. As he got angrier he got more silent; he would sit there, an unresponsive, unyielding block of wood against which I bruised myself and hammered in vain. It was I who made a fool of myself and danced about. Once I threw a book of Eugene O'Neill's plays at him and nicked a bit off the side of his forehead.

"Do you realise, Simon, that all our quarrels are about other people? If we were left alone we'd get on all right."

"God, how I hate people!"

"Well, only seven years more and then we'll go and live in the country and never see them. Meanwhile, what about Roddy?"

"If I go I'm sure to be damn rude to someone."

"Oh, all right."

I had a sudden idea. I went to the telephone and got a number.

"Savoy Hotel? Put me through to Mr. Marcus Chard, please. … Is that Mr. Chard? Nevis Falconer here."

"Why, this is nice of you," said Marcus Chard's voice.

He sounded so pleased, so sincere. For an instant I had a complete picture of him. I could see the thick lips close to the mouthpiece, the small brown eyes swallowed up by that network of good-humoured wrinkles. His heavy body would be balanced on the arm of one of those frail Louis Quinze chairs that they see fit to give you in hotel suites; beside him the cigarette would be smouldering in a glass ash-tray. I thought: "He's nice. I'd forgotten how much I liked him yesterday."

"I wondered if you were doing anything to-night?"

"Nothing that can't be put off right now."

"Would it amuse you to go to a party with me? Roddy Talent, the young man who designs stage sets and masks. It might be terribly dreary, or it might. … Yes, call for me here, about nine. … Oh, one of those parties where it doesn't particularly matter. Dinner-jacket, I should think."

"Why don't you come down here and dine with me first?"

"Well. …" Simon won't like it, and anyway I don't know that I want to, much. "… May I some other time?"

"Of course you may. All right, I'll be round at your place about nine."

"That's fine. Good-bye."

I went back to Simon.

"I'm taking Marcus Chard to the party to-night."

"Who's he?"

"Don't be a fool, darling. My American publisher."

"Oh!" He seemed to ponder.

"Is that all right?"

"Perfectly."

I looked at him and walked away. I went upstairs and sat down in front of my painted dressing-table and stared malignantly at the della Robbia Madonna. The tender colours, the divine embracing gesture of motherhood, were suddenly irritating. That was a virgin who knew nothing at all about life; her smile was as empty, as foolishly serene as the smile of a child or a half-wit. You could not imagine that the Christ in her arms had been torn from her body with blood and agony. She must have found him in a cold little blue egg under a lily-leaf. I thought, "I'll take the thing down." From somewhere a mood of unutterable wretchedness had sprung on me. If I could have thought of a good excuse I should have cried quite happily, but I could not think of one. I was alone in a vast, tired misery. This is what they call the artistic temperament, Gawd 'elp us!

> What is there left to do but die,
> Since Hope, my old companion,
> That something, something infancy. ...

Now who the hell wrote that? It sounds as though it might be Vaughan or Treherne. Or possibly George Herbert. "What is there left to do—" damn! Downstairs Simon started the gramophone.

"Simon! Si-mon!"

"What?"

"Turn that damn thing off!"

"What?"

I took down the Madonna and put her face downwards in a drawer among a jumble of peach-coloured chemises and stockings that wanted mending. The waltz out of *Bitter-Sweet* droned on.

❧

Marcus Chard and I had gone out on to the tiny balcony to have a cigarette. From where we leant against the rail we could see a slice of the room as though it were a modern drawing pinned against the darkness of the house wall; a warm, hazy, brown pit of shadows out of which someone's scarlet shoulder-strap emerged sharp as a crayon stroke; a jumble of bodies on the floor, turning tired faces towards the two grand pianos that were both being played rather well.

> "Moanin' low,
> My sweet man has *gorn* away. ..."

A quite famous comedian turned up. He leant against the piano and began to sing innocently dirty songs. His hair was a startling crimson; he looked bored to death. From the next room a cork popped loudly. There was a little burst of fresh animation.

"Play 'She's Such a Comfort to Me,' Billy."

"That's an old one. All right, here goes. But you must all sing."

The quite famous comedian said to a girl: "How divine you

look, darling, with your new hair. Every time I see you it's a different colour."

I leant against the rail, staring into the room, and thought: "My God, what a mess we all are!" I felt a return of the afternoon's wretchedness. The Kensington Square where Roddy lived was quiet and the trees in the garden stirred faintly. Near the railings was a bush of white lilac and a slim little tree of some sort of blossom. I could just make out its shape, slender and disdainful like a very young girl. The blossom would be wet against one's face, the bark cool and harsh to one's fingertips. ...

Simon was right to want to live in the country and keep horses and dogs. If one had a certain amount of money it was better to buy three or four of those beautiful, satisfying creatures than to spend it on buying gin for people who didn't matter a damn either way. I thought suddenly that Simon was the only real man I had ever known; the only man with guts instead of a polite little arrangement of guttapercha. Our generation doesn't seem to breed them that way. I thought, with a funny physical thrill of pleasure, of his hard body and his hard lips and the red-gold hair growing down from his wrists. If he came in at that door his realness would be appalling. He would look like a stag among a lot of does in boiled shirts.

Marcus murmured: "What are you thinking?"

"I was rather wishing that there could be another war."

"And turn the machine-guns this way?" He jerked his head towards the lighted room.

"Yes. It's all so damsilly, really."

"You're a bitter young person, aren't you?"

Roddy poked his head out and asked:

"What are you two doing? Nevis, I simply must have a little talk with you. What are you writing now, dear? You're so clever.

Isn't Simon coming? Do you know, darling, I don't believe that man likes me."

"Don't be absurd, Roddy."

"You're so sweet, you just say that. Lili Kasteliz ought to be here any moment now. Do you know her? She's Hungarian and acts in rather *awful* movies. I'm going to do a mask of her. All the French she knows is 'Je *suis très Internationale*,' and all the English she knows is 'Oh, how bloddy!' You'll love her."

He craned over the balcony. Every few minutes someone rushed out and cried, "There's Lili, but it always turned out to be the woman in the flat below or someone quite different. Inside they were playing again:

> "Moanin' low,
> My sweet man has *gorn* away,"

and it all got muddled up with that maddening tag of verse which had jigged in my head all the afternoon:

> What is there left to do but die,
> Since Hope, my old companion. …

> "He's the kinda man
> Needs a
> Kinda woman—
> Like—me—"

I threw my cigarette out into the square and repeated:

"So damsilly, really. Sorry, I'm not being amusing."

Marcus was between me and the room. All I could see of him was the outline of his big, clumsy head and his hands resting on the balcony rail full in the light. Funny how I always noticed those hands of his first of all. They were fascinating with their long dark fingers and pudgy palms. I looked at them and thought: "I wonder what sort of man you are really. I wonder how many women you've seen naked. Why in hell do I try to write books, when everyone's mind is such a dark, impenetrable mystery?"

"I'm wondering just what you're going to do with life, Nevis."

"I wish I knew." My laugh sounded deadly flat, as though it were some heavy bit of furniture that I couldn't make an effort to lift.

"Do you know where I think you're making a mistake?"

"All over the place. I'm just one walking mistake."

"You're just one walking fraud. You're trying like hell to be hard-boiled and tough and knowledgeable, when really you're very young and about forty times more sensitive than other people. Am I right?"

I felt angry and blustering and frightened. He was being so horribly right that it seemed almost indecent; it gave me the feeling of being stripped suddenly in an East wind. Not really comfortable or flattering. "Just one walking fraud. ..." I reminded myself that at the beginning I had not cared for the expression of his eyes. Too shrewd, too brightly and unpleasantly penetrating; not kind eyes, until he turned on that benevolent smile snap, like an electric light. But also, obscurely, I was fascinated. The fright and the fascination and the desire to bluster myself into a more becoming light in his mind were so confused that all I could manage was a muttered:

"Perhaps."

"That's what puzzled me in *Vulcan's Harvest*, and now I get it. You were trying to put over a fraud on yourself." A note of exasperation crept into his voice. "Why you, of all people, should kid yourself that you really wanted to make a study of a sour old spinster chock-full of sexual inhibitions and God knows what—"

My laughter was real this time.

"You don't think that inhibitions are in my line?"

"I do not."

"Oh!"

"I should say that you are a young woman who knows what she wants, and gets it."

"I wanted to marry Simon. I was very much in love with him. I still am. But sometimes I have a horrid feeling that marriage has cooked my writing. Not that it matters particularly." I stood up and laughed. "For God's sake let me pull myself together and try to be amusing. You're having a rotten evening."

"From now on," said Marcus slowly, "I'm going to appoint myself as a kind of literary godfather and slave-driver. You need one, it seems to me. What are you writing now?"

"Nothing much. I've got vague plans for a new book."

"Will you tell me about it some time? I might be able to help work it out. Let's have dinner together quietly one night next week."

"I'd like that. You're being awfully nice to me."

Before he could answer, Roddy was excitably with us again.

"My dear, here *is* Lili at last. And Simon! Oh, Simon, I'm so glad you could come after all. Do have a drink. The drinks are in the next room, but I'm afraid all the pâté has gone. Isn't it awful? I got such a lot from Fortnum's, because I think it looks awfully rich and grand, don't you?"

There was Simon. There was Simon standing in the doorway, fair and dangerous-looking and cold about the eye, in tails and a red carnation. Roddy Talent, slim and deprecating, towered over him, but in some curious way Simon seemed to tower over Roddy. I thought again: "A stag among a lot of does in boiled shirts." He was also slightly and cheerfully tight.

We stepped into the room, over people's legs and empty Woolworth tumblers and one young man who was lying full-length with his head in the coal-scuttle. Marcus Chard's face had become polite and expressionless. I thought idiotically: "Dark people can hide what they're thinking so much better than fair people. Their faces seem to shut up like glossy little black boxes."

"'Lo, Nevis."

"I thought you weren't coming."

"Well, after you'd gone I went along for drinks with some chaps, so thought I might as well look in here."

I felt suddenly and absurdly nervous.

"Marcus, this is my husband."

They looked at each other and shook hands.

"I'm very glad to meet you."

"Sorry I wasn't there when you called to collect Nevis this evening." He sounded so sincere. A pity I knew that he'd shut himself into the downstairs lavatory the moment the front-door bell went. "Well, this party seems to be going all right."

He surveyed it through drooping lids.

"Whisky, Simon?"

"I'd rather have beer, if you've got it."

"There *is* some more pâté. Oh, I'm so relieved. Lili darling, you're looking marvellous."

"*Je suis très Internationale.*"

Lili had goldfish-coloured hair and lovely, liquid dark eyes with a spot of rouge in the corner of each, and a really perfect bosom which called attention to itself insistently through the thin white crêpe of her dress. She should have had a grant from the government to go about perpetually like Lely's lascivious beauties. She had an intellectual little arched nose and a coarse, stupid mouth, daubed preposterously with scarlet wax. I wondered which came out victorious in the saint *versus* guttersnipe battle of her face. Simon had a tremendous success with her. He said:

"I think films are damn awful, but I don't mind going to see yours. Come and lunch with me. What about Tuesday at Quaglino's?"

"Oh, how bloddy!" said Lili, wiping her hands on the tail of her crêpe dress.

"Kind of woman I like," said Simon.

"Marcus, have you had enough of this? I'm feeling a bit tired."

"I'll take you home."

"*Je suis très internationale*," said Lili cordially, screaming with laughter and catching Simon a good-natured slap on the cheek.

❧

Simon arrived home twenty minutes after I did. I was sitting in front of the dressing-table, in my pyjamas, wiping off the cold cream. If he saw me he would be sure to say automatically, "Why the hell do you put that muck on your face?" and just as automatically I would respond, "Yes, you'd be damn pleased if I didn't and I had a lousy complexion, wouldn't you?" I did not feel in the mood for those little domestic pleasantries. It had begun to rain. The street was quiet as a stone, the air was soft and cool in my flushed face as I opened the windows. Maybe

Roddy's whisky was too good. I don't know why I drink the stuff. I'd rather have an ice-cream soda any day than all the whisky in the world.

I got into bed and snapped out the table lamp. Simon was moving about in the dressing-room next door, dropping shoes with intense deliberation. Presently he came in without turning on the light, closed the door, and sat down on the bed. He had an uncanny faculty for moving about in the dark like an animal. His hand passed lightly over my body until it reached my face.

"Asleep, baby?"

"No."

"Tired?"

"Why did you come to Roddy's party after making all that row about it?"

"I don't know. ... I was a bit jealous of that damn American. Do you love me?"

"Thanks very much for speaking so charmingly of my friends."

"As a matter of fact, he seems all right. I liked him. Do you love me?"

"You're tight."

"No, I'm not."

"Yes, you are."

The absurd, undignified dialogue was over. I shook off his hand and turned over on my other side. The bed sagged. He was getting in. I lay and thought of Marcus Chard. I thought: "I'll start the book next week. I really will make an effort. I'll ... Leave me alone!"

"Take that silly thing off," murmured Simon.

"I want to go to sleep. No! You're tight."

"Take that thing off."

There was the thin sound of silk tearing. Marcus Chard, the book, everything went out of my head. The world stopped. That tiresome young woman Nevis Falconer seemed to stop. From a long way off someone who resembled her faintly looked at her with a kind of detached pity.

"Do you realise," asked Simon later, "do you realise how many of our quarrels end this way?"

I didn't want to realise. I knew only too well, and that was what seemed to me so awful—that this stranger in the dark, this hard, naked stranger in the dark, should have the power to make anything he liked of me. In the dark he was not Simon; the Simon I loved for all sorts of pleasant absurdities like the way he laughed and brushed his hair. In the dark he was just any kind of ruthless, inexorable force, without personality or name. A force that could transform me from anger to tenderness, from hostility to desire; from the individual Nevis Falconer, with her petty liking for Beethoven and clothes and Vermeer, her petty dislike of stupidity and mothers-in-law, to a sensitive and quivering instrument of pleasure.

What was that thing I was trying to remember this afternoon? "What have I left to do but die"—it's coming back to me now:

> Since Hope, my old companion,
> That trained me from my infancy,
> My Friend, my Comforter, is gone?

So damn appropriate. I never realised until this minute that hope had gone. The hope of ever being anything but a young woman who one day wrote a Rather Good Book. The hope of ever writing anything better than a R. G. B. The hope of

Getting Away (Destination vague). So, taking all things into consideration, what have I left to do but—no, not die. Live and be a good little Quinn. I laughed out loud. Simon made a sleepy, inarticulate sound of tenderness, and drew me closer. His heart sounded muffled and solemn under my cheek. A lonely and mysterious sound, the heart of a stranger beating close to one in the dark. And soon I too was asleep.

With a brazen clash of hot-water cans Katie came into the room, and, averting her eyes carefully from the bed, drew back the curtains from two squares of pale-blue sky.

VI

When Cora came to see me in June, bringing a great armful of syringa and snapdragons from the Red Court gardens, she looked at me in silence for a minute.

"Just what has happened to you, may I ask?"

"Why?"

"Well, you look so much better. You're lovely, Nevis." She narrowed her eyes and regarded me smilingly. "Is it some man?"

"Oh," I laughed. "What would you say if it was?"

"I should say how perfectly splendid, and God bless your funny heart. But, in a way, what a pity. Because Simon has more worth-while faults and qualities than any man I know. Give me a cigarette, darling."

"You needn't worry. It's nothing to do with a man."

"I'm glad."

"Somehow I don't believe there will ever be anyone but Simon, Cora. Doesn't that sound hellishly Victorian?"

Cora murmured:

"I don't know. Being Victorian has its points. And *did* they have such a bad time?"

"If I ever left Simon, it would be all my own damn fault, nothing to do with another man. No, it's just—oh, I don't know."

"You needn't bother about telling me. It was only vulgar curiosity and envy."

"I was trying to get the right words. I'm so much happier, Cora. In the spring everything seemed to go wrong."

"I know."

"The in-laws got on my nerves. And I was so damnably discouraged about my work that there were times when I wanted to bolt."

"Where to?"

"God knows. That's always what stops you—thinking about the silly practical things like luggage-labels and time-tables and forwarding letters. If it could be just one big satisfying gesture—"

"Take a lesson from me, Nevis. A woman who has run from big, satisfying gestures all her life. They're damn uncomfortable things to live up to, and they put lines into your face. That is why you find me at the age of thirty-eight quite resigned to middle age, three children, a good complexion and no lovers."

"No reason for resigning yourself to the last item, darling."

Cora looked at me thoughtfully for a minute. I was arranging the syringa in a green glass tank. She lay on the sofa watching me; her dress was black crêpe with amusing touches of white; her little monkey face looked out rather wistfully from a tight-fitting black straw cap edged on the forehead with white like a nun's coif. The emerald on her left hand was matched exactly by the big chiffon handkerchief that she had thrown down together with a scarf of silver foxes. I thought that her clothes were marvellous.

"Do you know, Nevis, I can think of dozens of reasons. Frank, firstly. Secondly, the sad fact that I don't really want a lover. And then all sorts of selfish, cosy, thirty-eightish reasons. Breakfast in bed. A placid mushroom existence. Decorating the church with the Vicar's sister, doing a little gardening, enjoying my food—"

I burst out laughing.

"It all sounds disgustingly materialistic to me."

Cora murmured faintly:

"Of course it is. Why not? Most of the nice things are. Well, long may the luggage-labels keep you off the big satisfying gestures, my dear. Satisfying they may be for the moment, but they ruin the digestion."

I had changed, and not only physically. Clearer eyes, a little less sharpness round the cheek-bones, a few extra pounds in weight, were only the signs of a slow mental process. I was changing a little every day. I was more sure of myself; it seemed to me that I had never before worked with such ease and certainty. Marcus Chard had threatened to appoint himself as a kind of literary godfather and slave-driver. It was only rarely that he appeared in the first role. Occasionally I got a pat on the head, a "That's not bad," or still more occasionally, "That's pretty good." But he was the most merciless slave-driver I have ever come across. His criticisms had the sting of a whip; my vanity curled up and died under it. I loathed criticism. I had been pleased to think myself a pretty good writer, and here was Marcus telling me cheerfully: "Don't kid yourself! You're a pretty good natural writer. You write as naturally as you breathe, but it doesn't necessarily follow that your breathing is going to benefit the world very largely. At the present minute you're threshing about looking for a style, and before you find it, you'll have to learn not to write loose, faulty English. You want to live a bit more, my child, and learn a very great deal more. Being a writer doesn't just mean sitting down and picking up a pen and leaving the rest to the Almighty."

I said bitterly:

"I'm surprised you think I'm worth saving."

"Maybe you're not. I'm taking the chance."

Once he succeeded in reducing me to angry tears. I tried to choke them down, but they oozed through my lashes and rolled miserably down my cheeks. It seemed to me that it was no use going on. I was not such a complete damn fool that I couldn't recognise the truth. I was just a facile, valueless writer, and I might as well resign myself to being a facile, valueless writer. And suddenly Marcus was sweet. He said:

"You've had the powder; here comes the jam. This thing that I've been picking to pieces for a solid half-hour is good. It's swell. In its way it is probably the best thing that you've ever done. Now, for God's sake, go home and write some more like it."

But more often he was brusque and ruthlessly unflattering. Sometimes I almost hated him; I was afraid of him because he seemed to read my mind so easily, and I did not altogether care for the sensation. He made me work harder than I had ever worked before. He made me read. I had thought myself fairly well read, but the extent of Marcus Chard's scholarship opened up an abyss of ignorance before me. And in between times he was the most delightful and inexhaustible of companions. We did all the things that I had not thought of doing for years. We went to Hampton Court on top of a 'bus, and had a watercress tea at the Mitre. We went to the Tate Gallery, and filled ourselves with lark-pudding at the Cheshire Cheese, and stood in the crowd watching the Life Guards come jingling, impatient ebony and silver and scarlet, down the Mall.

When Marcus went to Paris I missed him. But he was back

in two weeks, and we celebrated with the white satin Lanvin and dinner at the Embassy. He danced terribly badly and got more fun out of it than anyone I have ever known. People stared at him. In his way he was rather a striking-looking person, with his great head and his strong arched nose and the thick hair that sprang out of his forehead as though it possessed a separate life and vitality of its own. Two more Americans joined us. Louis Nathan, the novelist, a great bear of a man with kind eyes that looked strangely dilated by the strong lens of his iron-rimmed glasses; he had a muzzy, droning voice that made me think of a nib with a hair in it. The other man was a cartoonist whose name I did not catch.

The place was unbearably hot. Louis said: "Let's all go over to Orlov's hotel. This is the night of his concert. You know him, don't you, Marcus?"

"Yes, I got to know him rather well in California, last year. What do you think, Nevis?"

"I'd like it."

Louis lumbered to his feet.

"Let's go."

He caught hold of my arm and steered me to the door. He and I walked the few hundred yards to Orlov's hotel; Marcus insisted on bundling the cartoonist into a taxi. He was unbelievably lazy. That was why he was coarsening and thickening so rapidly; another few years would see his fine features submerged in a creeping tidal wave of fat.

The stripped pine walls, the roses, the glazed chintzes of Orlov's suite were nearly blotted out with people. And in the middle somewhere, Orlov himself. A pleasant young man with simple manners and wavy blonde hair and American shoulders; his light-blue eyes were naive and a little bewildered, like the eyes of a child who has been brought down from his bed to perform for the grown-ups. The concert had been, as usual, a triumph. Always his little Jewish accompanist was at his elbow, watchful and anxious. Presently he would take Orlov away and put him to bed; he treated the violinist in a manner at once affectionate and sharply peremptory.

Marcus was watching me.

"Enjoying this?"

"Yes."

I wondered if I could explain to him that this party had the spontaneous quality that Roddy's party had lacked, for all its careful informality of cushions on the floor and people getting up to do impromptu turns; the quality that I missed in those rather dreadful little dinners at Montpelier Place. This was the old flat again, and Proutie in plum-coloured velveteen and gay people talking, talking, talking, I opened my mouth to drink it in as one might open one's mouth to drink in gulps of cool, life-giving water. I had not realised quite how badly I had missed Marcus. It had been an awful week. On Tuesday one of those stupefying, soul-destroying family dinners at Prince's Gate; on Wednesday an evening with two of Simon's Good Chaps, male and female. The female Good Chap said to me:

"Fancy being able to write! How many words do you do a day? Do you know the end when you're at the beginning? I should think that the plot would be easy, but I shouldn't be able to manage all the little bits, conversation and all that. I had a dream the other day that would have made a lovely plot. Oh, I do envy you being able to write!"

I said rudely:

"Why? It's just like any other job—sweeping a crossing or adding up figures in a ledger. There's nothing particularly romantic about it. You work at fixed hours and relax at fixed hours. Often you're deadly tired; still more often you're bored and discouraged. The only difference between me and the girl who licks stamps in an office is that she gets paid regularly every Friday evening."

The female Good Chap laughed uncertainly and opened wide her lovely, stupid cow eyes. On the way home I said to Simon: "If you ever want to have those damn people to the house, please tell me, and I can make arrangements to go out that evening." And then there was a row. ...

I smiled at Marcus and said:

"This is a nice party."

Beside me was Louis Nathan, producing the most idiotic and charming and brilliant remarks in that droning voice of his. And there was perhaps the greatest violinist of his day, handing round a tray of smoked-salmon sandwiches and fussing nervously over the telephone for more ice. It got very hot. I put on fresh powder and lipstick for the second time. Presently people began to leave, until there were only eight of us left. "Perhaps we'd better beat it too, and let you get some sleep, Nikolay." The little Jewish accompanist wailed: "My God, somehow I have got to get him on that Golden Arrow Pullman to-morrow!" But Orlov had turned into the petulant child daring his nurse. No one was to go yet. It was only—he brought out a Cartier gold watch as thin as a shilling—it was only three o'clock. "But, Nikolay, how do you think I get you in shape for our concert in Paris—"

"That's all right. That's all *right*."

He sat down at the piano and played Viennese waltzes rather badly. It was a relief, Marcus murmured, to find that someone who was so nearly a god with a Strad tucked under his chin could become abruptly human at a Steinway. He imitated the little dogs barking at a circus—*yap, yap, yap!*—and a pianola belching out "The Rosary" with deadly mechanical exactness. I laughed until the muscles of my face felt stiff. Everything was gay and spontaneous and delightful. And then someone drew aside the curtains to throw away a match, and there was Piccadilly in the cool blue translucence of the early summer dawn. "My God, somehow I have to get him on that Golden Arrow Pullman this morning, and he has not yet packed, my God!"

The streets looked so pure, so clean. One had the feeling that one was seeing them for the first time without all the silly people getting in the way. The broad sweep of Hyde Park Corner had such space and dignity; there stood the giant men of bronze on the Artillery memorial, brooding in the cold dawn light. London, my London! Water hissed across the street in a creaming gush. The tall houses in Knightsbridge looked white and mysterious like houses in a back street of some stifling little tropical town. One could not realise that behind those staring windows slept excellent individuals who would come downstairs four hours later to eat crisp bacon and comment on *The Times*, and read out that Ruby did not care for Rapallo, after all. In the sky there were four pink feathers of clouds, and slowly, almost deliberately, the plaster bubble of the Oratory dome swam into view.

I looked at Marcus, beside me in the taxi. He was looking old and suddenly rather moody; there were dark brown bruises under his eyes. The air was limpid as spring water. I wanted to go home and wash my face and find myself running down a hill in Gloucestershire. I wanted to go home and write the world into a cocked-hat.

"It's been a nice party, Marcus."

I put a tentative hand in his and raised my face. I meant it to mean nothing … and suddenly it was meaning something. Or was I just a bit tight? The taxi was slowing down with a horrid grinding noise.

"Good-bye, Marcus."

"Good-bye."

I wish I knew if I was tight or not. A queer yellowish light on the stairs; the dawn coming through the holland blinds. Simon was asleep, lying diagonally, face downwards, across the bed. His hair was rumpled; his face was strangely innocent and helpless, the curves of cheek and lip were almost infantile. I took off my clothes quietly, but he was lying on my pyjamas, so I had to get into bed naked. He woke and asked:

"What time is it?"

"Five."

"Who brought you home?"

"Marcus."

"Oh! Why haven't you got any clothes on, you naked woman?"

He was unconscious again.

That was what puzzled me a little. Simon, normally so jealous, did not seem to resent this friendship in the least. If anyone else had brought me home at five in the morning he would have gone through the roof. But he got on excellently with Marcus; perhaps he saw that I was happier and more contented than I had been for two years.

Marcus never said anything about Simon. Sometimes I wondered what he thought of him. I did not ask.

❧

Sometimes I wondered what I thought about Simon. I would catch myself standing away from him mentally and thinking: "How exactly do I feel about you after three years?" And it would surprise and rather annoy me to find that I was still passionately in love with him. It would annoy me because the slight, fair-headed figure of Simon seemed to get between me and so many things. And it would surprise me because there were moments when I felt that something so mad and violent could not possibly last. It was like poor Juliet's love—

> ... too rash, too unadvis'd, too sudden;
> Too like the lightning which doth cease to be
> Ere one can say—It lightens.

Most people would have said that we had begun marriage at the wrong end; we had founded it simply and solely on sex attraction. By all the rules it should have begun to totter; instead, it had lasted. When we were not throwing Eugene O'Neill's plays and insults at each other's heads we were being gaily mad dog and recklessly, ecstatically happy.

Sunday was the day of the week when we were happiest and when I seemed to see Simon with the greatest distinctness. Week-days were all cluttered up with work and other people and, just lately, with Marcus. Simon and I were rarely alone; we were nearly always tired and often nervous and on edge. People who live in big cities get that way.

But Sunday was our day of rest. No one else was allowed to intrude upon it. However bitterly we had quarrelled on Saturday night, the quarrel was shelved on Sunday. Katie would stagger upstairs with our breakfast-trays at nine o'clock, and for two hours we lay in dreamy, voluptuous peace among crumbs of toast and stubs of pencil and the *Sunday Times* and cigarette-ends. Punctually at nine-fifteen the great battle of the *Sunday Times* would be fought. I wanted all the book reviews and James Agate and the picture-galleries; Simon wanted the racing news and the leader page and the Stock Exchange. The simple solution of ordering two copies never occurred to us.

Every Sunday we went into the country. We never went to church. Sometimes we got a couple of horses and rode. Sometimes we bought chocolate and bulged our pockets with oranges and walked for miles. Simon loved maps. He loved finding the old Roman trackways and the Celtic camps. His imagination could people them with men and horses, crawling babies and dogs sniffing about the walls, when all I could see was a chalk-scarred hill dotted with dark juniper-bushes and ridged with strange bumps and circles. I would be conscious only of the cold wind up my legs while Simon stood with his head thrown back, muttering angrily: "My God, those were the days to be born in!"

It was better fun looking for nice and amusing names. Britwell Salome, Aston Tirrold, Winterbourne Basset, Drunken Bottom, Nether Wallop.

Simon swore that there was a village called Chipping Bastards and that one day we would go and live there.

"Yes, do let's, Simon. It will be such fun saying to people 'I do want you to come down to our little place at Chipping Bastards.'"

"Telegraph address, 'Illegitimate,' I suppose."

And we wove preposterous legends about Chipping Bastards. It was like Drinkwater's Mamble. "I've never been to Mamble. That lies above the Tame, so I wonder what's in

Mamble. …" Thatch was never thicker and more mossy than on the Chipping Bastards cottages. Clean old men in smocks drank their beer outside a low white inn up which a vine spread its arms, and in the big Tudor house on the hill a mad squire sat listening, with a ruined smile, to the screaming of his peacocks. In the gardens they grew only the sweet old flowers: gillystocks, phlox, Sweet Williams, sops-in-wine. Nowhere in the world was there a more delicious place than Chipping Bastards in which to spend one's days.

I liked watching Simon in the country. A profound peace would come into his face as he reined in his horse and sat, relaxed in the saddle, looking down at the silvery autumn fields and the poplars trembling against a sky of rolling clouds, the little farms wreathed in a haze of wood smoke. And dimly I would comprehend the secrets of content that he knew and I did not know; I would understand the calm and enduring England of which he was a part. And I would derive a strange satisfaction from the thought that there would always be men who sat on their horses and looked down with quiet eyes at fields like these. It kept one's balance, somehow.

Just about that time we got the dog that Simon had threatened for so long. One of the Good Chaps bred him for us. James was a Scotch terrier. He had one peculiarity: he would lie for hours with his front part on the ground and his back part well pushed up in the air. Simon said unkindly that he reminded him of Roddy Talent. Sunday was James's particular day, too. On week-days he waddled mildly round the shops on a lead, existing until six o'clock when Simon's key rattled in the door. In his heart that dog despised me. When I stopped to look in a window, James would subside heavily and crack his face in two with a yawn as though to say: "Oh, God, another shop! Well, when you've finished looking there, do you mind if I have a sniff here? No? Darn it, who was the guy who wrote that bit about a dog's life?"

But Sunday was a man's day. No shops, only rabbit-holes; no pavements, only coarse grass where cowslips nodded on tough pinkish stalks; exciting and dangerous as a primeval jungle. May passed, and with it some of the shining freshness of buttercups and brilliant green and apple-blossom tumbling over orchard walls in a pale cataract. Now it was June, and the lavender bushes in cottage gardens were beginning to bristle like hedgehogs with purple quills. There were long evenings and beautiful green dusks that made a hurt angry feeling come into my chest. Gorse was a scalding gold on the commons, and when we walked there the air was sweet as crushed almonds.

Simon lay on his back on the grass, staring up at a copper beech tree. He could lie for hours watching a tree or a horse in a field or a bird, quite happy and intent. In the woods James hunted and screamed, losing native caution in blood-lust. And I watched Simon, sitting with my back against the great trunk and the wind running fingers through my hair. He was wonderful to watch on a horse, but equally wonderful just lying there with the shadows of the beech leaves making a pattern on his face. The dusty gold of his hair seemed to blend in with the grass; between those light flickering lashes was the sky.

"Do you know that little poem, 'Lost in France,' Simon? No, of course you don't."

"Say it."

"I'll try to remember. Let's see. ...

"He had the plowman's strength
In the grasp of his hand.
He could see a crow
Three miles away,
And the trout beneath the stone.
He could hear the green oats growing,
And the sou'-west making rain. ...
And plow as straight as stone can fall.
And he is dead."

"I like that. Say it again, Nevis."
I said it again.
"Yes," said Simon, slowly, savouring it. "Yes."
"It reminds me of you, Simon. I do believe that you can hear the green oats growing and the sou'-west making rain."
"I can see a crow damn nearly three miles off. Look, there he goes."
I followed the tiny black speck with my eyes as it flapped away into the distance. There was not a house in sight, only the rolling little English hills, the darkness of ploughed land and the hay standing high. Two brimstone butterflies whirled past. There was a glitter, a soft, lazy hum. ...
"My God, Simon, why don't we live in the country?"
"Because of you."
"But it's so divine, really."
"You think so on Sundays. If I suggested it to-morrow you'd say"—he gave a very tolerable imitation of a querulous feminine voice. ... "'How the hell do you think I'd ever get any copy stuck down there?' What you want is someone to beat you."
He rolled over on his face and buried it abruptly in the grass, making deep grunting sounds of content.

"God, that's good! Ever done that? You can hear the earth breathe and the beetles stamping about like cart-horses."

"Only seven more years, Simon."

"And then?"

"We'll buy a cottage at Chipping Bastards and I shall write a strong, earthy book that will win the Femina Prize."

"No." He raised his head and shook it. "You'll have left me by then."

"What do you mean?"

He collapsed again, face downwards.

"Simon!" I spoke sharply; for some reason I felt lonely and afraid.

"I thought that you knew it," he said in a muffled voice.

"Knew what? Don't be an ass!"

"All right, I'm being an ass." He sat up and gave me a brilliant, disarming smile. "Don't look so frightened. What are you looking frightened about?"

"I don't know."

I was suddenly very miserable. I lay on my back and stared up at the copper beech tree. It rose in such a miraculous pyre of weaving branches and smooth bronze leaves, high, high, until it lost itself in darkness. Right at the core was a lozenge of blue sky. What was the use of trying to write? I could expend years of energy, gallons of ink, without conveying to anyone else exactly how this tree glowed with secret dark fire in the sunlight, how the trunk stretched out snaky limbs, strong and delicate and exact, to support the piled magnificence of the leaves. Piled magnificence—words, words! What was the good of them? I wanted a new medium, something between writing and painting, with scents and sounds thrown in. How can I make someone see this copper beech tree, smell the cool, luscious grass, hear the hum of bees in the red and purple vetches? It's no good. ...

I rolled over on my side. Wild clouds were scudding over the sun. At one moment a field would shine out; a moment later it would have been swallowed up by the silent shadow, and far ahead travelled the moving finger of light tearing a haggard brilliance from the earth. Now it was poison-green, now brown with a purple bloom along the furrows, now cold silver streaked with shadows of wind. Only the pine woods on the opposite fold of hill preserved their mystery, their dense, unrelenting gloom. I stared at them and felt acutely miserable.

Simon asked:

"Did you say anything to Hilda about dinner at home to-night?"

"I don't know. ... No."

"Well, what about going to—" and he named the little river pub overlooking the weir. We had never gone back again.

"All right."

"What's the matter?"

"I don't know."

"You don't seem to know the hell of a lot, do you?"

"Oh, leave me alone!"

But presently I began to smile, and then to laugh. It was impossible to be miserable for very long on a Sunday. Simon said mildly:

"My God, you are a little rotter. You've got the filthiest temper of any woman I know. Come on, let's go."

He dragged himself reluctantly to his feet. We whistled for James and walked slowly to the car, casting lingering glances at the woods and fields. The sun had run far away by now. It was striking a thin gilt brightness from a row of poplars that stood by themselves, teetering gingerly on the crest of a sharp hill.

"Which would you rather have, flowers or trees?"

"Trees."

"So would I. Simon, one day we *will* live in the country."

He laughed.

"I don't know why you're laughing, Simon."

By the time we got to the little pub it was dark. The river looked darkly, oilily green, and the garden swam in green light. There were the three tubs filled with staring marguerites. Below us the weir still thundered its tale of doom as it gushed creaming into the quiet river, dissolved and flowed gently, docilely between the queer little stunted dwarfs of willows.

"Just the same, Simon."

"Yes."

He stood with bent head, sleepily looking at the river; he was smiling to himself. I thought, "after all, nothing else matters but this," and I slipped a hand through his arm. We stood in silence. The silence was deep, green, oily; not even a bird broke it. Behind us the herbaceous border was a pale cloud in the green air.

"I'm glad nothing has changed. I couldn't have borne it if a thing had been different."

But when we went inside the little pub we found change. Someone had discovered it. The lounge was full of chintzes and horribly twisted oak; a young man in a white coat stood shaking dry Martinis behind a spick-and-span little bar. There were no quiet middle-aged men smoking pipes, but there was a babel of sharp, brittle voices, and an Old Etonian tie leant against the bar, plucking its Adam's apple and saying, "By God, that's damn funny! That's damn funny!" Then it would laugh windily with the sound of a rubber pig expiring. Three whores sat crossing their knees and looking complacently at the tips of their brown and white shoes.

Only the stuffed salmon had survived the shadow of change. Its glazed eye seemed to catch mine pathetically, as though to say, "What in God's name are we coming to, a respectable fish like me?" Outside the leaded window-panes the garden stirred secretly in the luminous green light; the gnats danced low over the river. There was a great bush of syringa near the old boat-house. One could walk quietly through the long grass and hold the branches against one's cheek; the leaves would be faintly moist with dew, the blossom heavy with sweetness. And one would stay there for a long time, happy, motionless. ... One crossed one's knees and said, "I'll have a dry Martini."

One whore said to another whore:

"Have you been to Bray, dear?"

"Oh, yes. Bray's lovely. Bray's awfully nice."

"This place seems rather dead-and-alive. Of course it's awfully quaint, isn't it? But it might give me the pip after a bit."

"That's damn funny! That's damn good, by God!" said the Old Etonian tie.

He raised his head in the attitude of a hen drinking, and gently, coaxingly massaged his Adam's apple. Then, as though to take it by surprise, he swallowed a glass of sherry at a gulp and, catching sight of Simon, said:

"Hallo, Quinn!"

"How are you," said Simon in his most blandly insulting voice.

I felt angry and depressed. This place had stood for something precious and perfect; now it was spoilt, invaded, desecrated. The brown and white shoes had found it out. All the whores in London would come down in Mercedes cars and walk in our garden and smell our syringa and listen to our weir. They would be brought here for the weekend by blonde young men with suede shoes and spots on their chins. They would repeat in horrible travesty, perhaps in the very same low-ceilinged room, all the outward gestures and symbols of that night.

With difficulty I restrained a sudden desire to be sick.

We dined in a room that was almost *too* old-world, *too* cute, *too* cluttered up with warming-pans and sporting prints and pewter pepper-pots. Wherever the eye turned there was a warming-pan. "God!" said Simon gloomily, looking at them. I remembered a good, solid Victorian sideboard on which had been ranged four immense cruets and a vast silver dish-cover; that, too, had disappeared. The new proprietor leant over our table and purred, "Is everything all right?" It might have been the Ritz.

Simon was watching me over the table (electric candles shaded by parchment Cries of Old London, absolutely *too* attractive for words).

"You're depressed."

"Yes. One oughtn't to come back to a place where one has been happy. It's always a risk, always depressing."

"I know."

In the next room someone started a gramophone. And suddenly, ridiculously, we were in the middle of a violent quarrel. We were venting on each other our anger with those insufferable squawking people, these preposterous warming-pans. The original thread of the argument was so frail that we lost sight of it almost at once. The quarrel ranged freely back into the past and forward into the future; it embraced my friends, Simon's tastes, and mutual unsuitability for marriage.

"Oh, you're perfectly hopeless!"

And Simon pushed back his chair with a harsh, grating noise, nearly wrecking Cherries, Ripe Cherries.

"For God's sake let's get out of this place."

While he paid the bill I walked out into the garden. No one had come out yet, but the gramophone still brayed and brayed. Oh, yes, Bray's lovely. Bray's awfully nice. The familiar river smell was bitter-sweet, dank, rotten. A blanched moon was racing rapidly through the sky, turning the flat meadows to silver gilt, the willows to malignant hunchbacks crouching in shadow.

We had been lovers here, and we had come back saying cruel, senseless things to each other. It should have been quiet, tranquil, full of memories, and it had ended in the scrape of a chair and "For God's sake let's get out of this place!" What was it all about, anyway? I can't remember. How beastly life is! One spoils everything for oneself. Everything! The moon blurred, the meadows seemed to be covered in fine, shining mist. I couldn't find a handkerchief.

Simon came up behind me.

"What are you thinking about?"

He pushed back the short hair from my ear and very gently bit it. Oh, these battles, these armistices, how exhausting they are! I was too exhausted to do more than turn in his arms and whimper miserably, defensively:

"It was all your fault."

"I daresay it was. Damned silly, anyway."

"Don't let's come here again, Simon."

"All right. Poor baby, you're so tired. Come home and I'll put you to bed."

Well, there's another thing spoilt. Simon's right. I have got the filthiest temper. But it *was* all his fault. Or was it? Somehow I'm so tired … it doesn't seem to matter. …

VII

Granny died in July. We both went up to Gloucestershire for the funeral, which depressed me very much. Aunt Lorna was there, and all the uncles and cousins. Everyone looked strange and uncomfortable in their black clothes. Aunt Lorna's pale face was puffy and discoloured with crying; it came to me as quite a shock that she would miss Granny and was sorry that the old woman was dead. I remembered how my grandmother used to shout: "Lorna, you're a fool. And an old maid. Can't abide fools or old maids!" Yet there was my aunt sniffing quietly into her handkerchief instead of lighting bonfires and dancing about in the road. I had a sudden impulse to be very kind to her. I told myself that we would have her up to stay with us and somehow, in one indignant week, make up for a dreary and uncomplaining lifetime spent as a safety-valve for Granny's temper. In my heart I knew that we would do nothing of the sort, and that if we did it would be more than futile. Theatres and breakfast in bed every morning as a return for Aunt Lorna's wasted youth! But it made me feel better momentarily.

It was odd how all the personality had gone out of the funny little stucco house. It seemed stagnant, waiting to hear the peremptory summons of Granny's bell startle the hot afternoon silence. We sat in the drawing-room, that familiar jumble of *pot-pourri* bowls, huge photographs of my father in full uniform, tiger-skins and all the Indian junk that she had collected in my grandfather's soldiering days. Now that her fierce old personality was not there to bind them into some sort of harmonious whole, that was what they seemed. Junk. Already the room had the purposeless air of an auction-sale; one looked for the Lot tickets on the water-colour sketches and the grinning brass idol. Aunt Lorna would go on living here until she died, and then, this queer collection of stuff would be broken up; the little house and the old lilac-bush that we loved as children would go finally out of our lives.

All the old servants from Falconer Court had turned up for the funeral. I reflected grimly that Mrs. Quinn's feudal Tracy-Yarborough mind would be pleased at this. It was stiflingly hot. The grass in the churchyard had just been cut; it smelt cool and sweet. The air was showered with the song of birds, and over the wall leant a rose-bush covered with velvety bright red roses. It seemed to shout "Life! Life! Life!" The smell of newly-turned earth was strong and vigorous, and that, too, instead of shouting "Death! Death!" shouted "Life! Life!"

"He cometh up, and is cut down like a flower; he fleeth as it were a shadow, and never continueth in one stay."

I could not bring myself to feel very sorry. Death seemed something fantastic and improbable when all round us was hot, teeming life, the smell of grass and earth. Aunt Lorna was crying softly. By turning my head slightly I could see over the low churchyard wall into the fields, and there was one farm cat chasing another farm cat with lust in its eye; a black shadow slinking on its belly after a red shadow into the grasses. Cats, men, life! So we go on.

I looked at Simon and thought how fair and taut he looked among the cousins, who were nearly all dark, with big, loose-jointed bodies, I remembered Granny telling him that he would be the runt of the family, and the thought flashed wildly through my head: "I wonder if they've buried her with her false hair on." Granny fleeing as it were a shadow, with her false hair and her best set of teeth—the idea was so grotesque that I nearly laughed.

But in the train going home I was depressed. It was sad, somehow, saying good-bye to the little white house. I didn't think that I would go there again. It had been a lovely garden for children's games, with the great frightening cypress-tree and the broken swing; then there had been the famous lilac-bush, and next to it the bush of greenish-white snowballs, and the snapdragons had snapped so beautifully. ...

"Horrid business burying someone, Simon. A little of oneself is buried too."

Directly we got home I rang up Marcus. I had not seen him for five days and that was too long. It was amazing how large a portion of my life had come to be filled by his broad, clumsy figure. But the telephone said:

"Sorry, madam. Mr. Chard is away. He left for Paris yesterday."

"Oh! For how long, do you know?"

"I couldn't say, madam."

"All right."

I felt let down, and my face showed it as I went back to Simon.

"Wasn't he there?"

"Gone to Paris."

Simon was silent. I sat down crossly on the sofa and hated the green of the walls.

"He might have left a message for me, I think."

"When is he going back to America?"

"I don't know."

It was the first time that I had thought of the idea seriously, and it left a nasty cold feeling in the pit of my stomach. We were sitting in the dusk, with all the windows open; it was a stiflingly hot evening. The lamplighter had just come along, and the little street was a quiet pastel. I felt unbearably sad. In the house with the lettuce-green door a gramophone was playing Rhapsody in Blue. All these funny little rabbit-hutches with their red doors, their green doors, their brass knockers; all these funny little rabbits huddled inside, nibbling their evening lettuce; quarrelling, playing gramophones, and reproducing themselves; turning up their funny little toes to the daisies. ... What a damn muddle life is, and will Hilda remember that I said coffee for breakfast to-morrow?

I thought with a kind of futile, childish rage how nothing stays the same. To-day it had been good-bye to the little white house and the lilac-bush and young Nevis with her black pigtails. There they were, streaming away from me as relentlessly as a train moves out of a station. Soon it would be good-bye to Marcus and this particular phase of Nevis Falconer. They too would be round the bend. I thought of Marcus and the dawn ending of Orlov's party. For the first time I thought of him physically, and it struck me that many women would find him attractive; his slow, deliberate movements and curious hands; his broad shoulders and strong white teeth. For some reason I did not want to go on considering the physical aspect of Marcus Chard, and I got up restlessly to get a cigarette.

Over the road they had changed the record.

"What is that thing—
Called—

Love—
What is that. ..."

There was a burst of laughter from the pub at the corner. Simon stirred and looked wistfully out of the window. Up in Gloucestershire, I thought, Granny is lying under a quilt of flowers, and those bright red roses will be looking black in the twilight. Marcus is in Paris, damn him. Katie is moving about heavily overhead, turning back the beds. The King is in Buckingham Palace; James is whining in his sleep; in the folds of the Sussex Downs the night must be gathering in pools and the woods coiled up like a dark sleeping animal. Who cares? In another hundred years all will be gone, smashed, dust, so far as I am concerned.

And I wished with passionate misery that I were seven years old again, for then it had seemed so impossible that life would ever change; that Mother would ever die, or the summers at the little white house come to an end; that the lilac would flower for the last time, or that Granny's bell would not always summon us helter-skelter from the hay-loft and the swing under the cypress tree.

※

Simon's yearly holiday began in the first week of August. Every year we argued fiercely as to how and where those fourteen days should be spent; by the time they arrived I was usually so exhausted that I would have gone quite docilely to Southend. Unfortunately our ideas of a good holiday were not the same. Simon liked to motor very fast from place to place, pausing occasionally to climb something or ride something or fish for something. I liked to be hopelessly lazy in one place. I liked to swim and doze in hot sunlight, to lie for long hours with a book which I had no intention of reading, but I liked to be able to emerge at will and find people waiting for me, ready to be watched and speculated about until I grew tired of civilisation and returned to the wilderness again. But Simon said: "People! My God, the whole point of a holiday is to escape from people, as fast and as far as you can." So one year we had motored in Devonshire, the next in Ireland. ...

This year he had managed to get an extra week, and after a great deal of impassioned discussion we had decided to take the car abroad and motor down through the Black Forest to Venice. Neither Simon nor I had ever been to Venice. It would be wonderful to discover it together; I felt dimly that if we were alone for a bit in all that beauty we should come back mysteriously refreshed and enriched for another year in London. And it would be my kind of holiday. There would be the swimming and the hot sun; possibly music; certainly, dark, cool churches in which to sit and look at pictures; certainly abounding life and beauty and thin palazzos standing like shadows in the kind of aquamarine twilight that Guardi loved to paint. I felt that I could afford to be generous, and I said to Simon that we might stay a couple of nights in the Engadine and climb several large mountains. He cheered up at that, and shouted down the kitchen stairs to Katie to find his nailed boots.

There was always the possibility that Simon would spoil Venice for me. He was not very good at being a foreigner; abroad, he became maddeningly Quinnish. We had only tried the experiment once, and that had been a disastrous four days in Paris, after which we had quarrelled violently and I had come home alone. Directly Simon set foot on the quays at Calais his hair seemed to get brighter, his lips more aggressively stubborn; he would speak to the porters and the taximen in English with the slow, malignant clearness that one reserves for the half-witted, and then be annoyed because they did not understand him. But for some reason I had a feeling that nothing Simon could do would spoil Venice for me. Not even an army of Quinns flying banners could do that.

I was glad that I was going away before Marcus came back. There was still no word from him, and I was hurt; I thought it odd that he should go off like that without even coming to say good-bye. Perhaps he had decided to pick up a boat at Cherbourg and I shouldn't see him again. I didn't ring up the Savoy to find out. Everything seemed too much effort just then; I had that lax, end-of-the-summer feeling. London was hot and smelt stale. Like the heroine of an Edwardian novel it had "slipped on something loose," and was taking slovenly ease in the *negligée* of drawn holland blinds and empty window-boxes, dusty trees, slowly-moving crowds, theatres closed for re-decoration. In the parks tired men in shirt-sleeves lay about on the grass, sleeping the office poison out of their systems; dirty children sucked lemonade out of a bottle as they squatted under the heavy, exhausted green clots of the chestnut branches. I couldn't work. Simon said that the office was dead. It would be good to get away.

I went to see Gwen before we left. She was looking rather ill; her figure was unwieldy and distorted in one of those maternity frocks with artful jabot fronts that conceal not, neither do they thin.

"Are you pleased?"

"Oh, I suppose so, in a way. But it's such a beastly nuisance, feeling rotten and looking like a sack of potatoes. The doctor says that it's going to be earlier than we thought—that's one blessing, anyway."

I looked at the clear, colourless oval of her face, the transparent blue ice of her eyes between their thick curling lashes. Ice, yes; but ice that had retained its clarity and its dazzling brilliance, yet had miraculously become gentle. Gwen's eyes and lips were wonderfully gentle. I thought how strange it was that this childish creature should have anything to do with passion and the slow processes of birth. I tried to think of her and Adrian together, quarrelling, making silly jokes, sleeping in the same bed. It seemed incredible, impossible, absurd. Perhaps Adrian had had nothing to do with it and Gwen had been lover to a milk-white swan, a shower of gold, a pillar of fitful elfin fire. ... I came back with a start. Gwen's high, clear voice asked:

"What are you thinking about?"

"You."

"Me? What are you thinking about me?"

"How funny it was that you should have two children and be going to have a third."

"Oh, I don't know. It gives me something to do. If I didn't have Colin and Tim there'd be nothing but going out to lunch and playing bridge and buying clothes. ... Now you"—she looked at me rather shyly ... "it's different with you, of course, Nevis. You're so busy and so clever. I envy you sometimes."

"But not often."

"No, not very often."

She gave a contented little smile, and for a moment I felt the envy of which she had just spoken. I was not to be envied, but Gwen was to be envied. Life was so easy for her, so calm and safe. She knew what she wanted, she knew her own limitations.

"It's different with you, of course, Nevis." I couldn't imagine myself making that admission to anyone; but Gwen was full of humility. She often said in that placid little voice of hers, "I'm such a *frightful* fool, you know," and her laugh would rob the statement of any suspicion of bitterness.

Yes, Gwen was to be envied. She would never be intensely happy or intensely miserable. She would never be exalted to the skies and cast down in the darkness of hell as I was alternately exalted and cast down; her life would move graciously in an even climate of content. And I thought, "That is a very good thing." I thought, "Gwen is cleverer than you are." For her quiet, self-contained happiness showed me how unimportant the Quinns really were. I had exaggerated them out of all proportion into the symbol of everything I detested and feared, but to Gwen they were just Adrian's family—irritating at times, perhaps, but nothing more—who had to be given Christmas presents and asked to dinner once or twice a month. She sat in her home, she lived her mysterious, not-to-be-contemplated life with Adrian, and she was happy. That was a very good thing, and something to be remembered for comfort when I was next struggling with the powers of darkness.

"It gives me a nice settled feeling, coming to see you, Gwen."

"Well, aren't you settled?"

"Not really. I've got a house of my own and a parlourmaid and a dog, but it doesn't make me feel permanent. I'm terribly restless, I'm afraid."

"I should think that being on your own, like you were before you married Simon, would make it rather difficult to settle down."

"It may be that. ... Do you know, I don't believe that Mrs. Quinn has ever really got over that flat of mine. She thought it *so* immoral to have no parents and live over a garage in the King's Road."

Gwen laughed. There was a silence, out of which she asked unexpectedly:

"Are you happy, Nevis? You and Simon, I mean. I've often wondered."

Gwen had often wondered. It gave me a passing shock, as it does when one happens to overhear oneself discussed by other people. It is quite possible and seemly that I should waste a little malicious wit at my friends' expense, but it is out of the question that they should employ the same tone in speaking of me; that they also should have their private surmises and curiosities and jokes about me. In the strange little world that went on behind the glacier-blue of her eyes Gwen had speculated and pondered.

"Yes. I think so. It's rather difficult to say, isn't it?"

"It isn't for me. I know I'm happy. But then I don't really think very much."

She said it so quaintly, and the quaintness sat with such an odd effect on the child's face above the woman's body that I burst out laughing.

"Gwen, you're so funny, and such a darling."

"Well, isn't it better to be a fool? I know you all think I'm terribly stupid, but if I wasn't Adrian and I would be fighting all the time. There has to be someone who gives in, and it's never Adrian. He's terribly strong-willed." For a moment her mouth and eyes looked disconcertingly shrewd. "Simon's like that too, isn't he? All the family are alike in that way."

"Yes." I thought of Adrian again; this time, with faint alarm and amazement, in connection with Simon. It was always difficult for me to think of them as brothers. Physically they were so different, although at times their light eyes and the shape of their heads gave them a faint blood resemblance to one another. Yet they were alike; a thousand mysterious ties, of which I knew nothing, held them. Adrian had known Simon for twenty-eight years before I began to love him, and in those "Do you remembers?" I could have no part. I had seen Adrian put a hand on Simon's shoulder now and then, and they spoke of each other with light, sardonic affection. They were brothers. They stood together in a mysterious little circle into which I could not come.

I looked at Gwen, and tried again to think of her with Adrian. I thought, "Because she loves Adrian she must love a part of Simon, and because I love Simon I must love a part of Adrian." Horrible thought! She moved, and a trick of the light made her look strained and sallow. Really, it's an abominable business, all this nature. Why can't we lay a nice egg and take it in turns to sit on it for nine months?

She said:

"You've got a pretty firm chin yourself, Nevis. Look at mine; it's simply disgusting. Aren't there things for developing chins like they do busts?"

She got up and stood looking down at me. Her lips were grave, folded lightly together, but her amazing eyes smiled; such kind eyes, empty of everything but gentleness and blinding, drenching colour. Perhaps she was right. It was better to be a fool and to have a simple heart. I knew that I should not think so for long, and that presently I should be saying with affectionate contempt that Gwen was a little idiot to let Adrian have his own way all the time, but at the moment simplicity seemed more important than the ability to store up scraps of useless information about people and places and things; kindness was more desirable than a certain turn for light, malicious wit. And wasn't Gwen justified in doing nothing but just continuing beautifully to be? There was no physical magnetism about her; she set no sparks of imagination alight; but one took a quiet pleasure in looking at her as one looks at a flower and takes pleasure in its soft, pure colouring and its springing grace.

She said:

"I don't believe you're the kind of person who'll ever find it easy to be happy. You want too much, Nevis. Not like me. I haven't a scrap of ambition and I just jog along."

"You're lucky."

"Yes, I believe I am. I've got Adrian and Colin and Tim. Come and see the infants, by the way, if it won't bore you."

She looked at me in a shy, rather deprecatory way. I got up quickly.

"Of course it won't bore me, Gwen."

"Well, I hope they're not yelling." She led the way to the door. With her hand on the knob, she said casually in that cool little voice: "Do you know that I used to be rather frightened of you, Nevis? I can't think why."

"*Were* you?"

"Yes, a bit. You were so lovely and so damn clever, it didn't seem fair, with me being such a fool." She laughed cheerfully. "Of course I'm not now. I think you're one of the most unfrightening people I know. Isn't it silly?"

I said severely: "Yes, very, Gwen," but I reached out and squeezed her arm.

We went into the nice hygienic blue nursery and watched Colin and Timothy playing on the nice hygienic cork floor. They were well-mannered children, light-eyed and straw-coloured, like Adrian. I watched them with curiosity and interest. Something that had been a cell plasm, a blind lump of jelly, a mouthless parasite, was sitting on the floor waving a toy motor menacingly over the head of another ex-parasite. In the room, invisibly, was a third parasite, still coiled happily in the darkness of Gwen's body. Granny mouldering in Gloucestershire earth, cats chasing each other into the grasses, parasites hatching in darkness. So mysteriously and absurdly and inexplicably, we go on.

"Careful," said Gwen, and took the toy motor out of her elder parasite's hand.

Timothy climbed into my lap. His little body was firm and round. He smelt faintly of milk and sweet powder; as he panted laughter into my face I could see the little red cavern of his mouth and the teeth showing like kernels of wheat. Funny to think that this beautiful small being, perfect down to the last finger-nail and curl of moist fair hair, would grow into a man who made snoring noises in his sleep and desired women and thought all kinds of base and beautiful thoughts.

Colin came and stood beside us.

"Be a horse," he urged me. "I want to play horses."

Gwen laughed.

"Isn't he like Adrian?"

Yes, he was going to be very like Adrian, with his narrow head, his light eyes, his thin arched nose that reminded one so comically of the nervous, highly-bred animals that he loved. The Quinn ego was relentless. There would always be Quinns. I looked at Gwen and hoped that the unborn child would be like her, so exactly like that there could be no mistake, but with icy-blue eyes that were not tempered with gentleness. Gentleness was no good in making a stand against the Quinns. I hoped that the child would be a girl who would grow up into a wild creature with an un-Quinnish urge to write bad books in a garret, or become a movie star or run off with the leader of a tango band.

And then the door opened and Mrs. Quinn came in. She did not rustle, but one felt that she ought to have rustled, dryly and irritatingly, like bamboos in a hot wind. There was always that feeling of nervous fret and fever about her. I discovered suddenly that she had absolutely no talent for repose; it was impossible to imagine her sitting with folded hands, doing nothing but quietly thinking. Mrs. Quinn never thought to no purpose, and her hands, thin and dry-looking, were always plunged into a mass of grey wool that was destined to be a golf stocking for old Edward. In the evenings the stockings made way for the more refined *gros point*; every chair in the Prince's Gate house testified to that remorseless, indomitable energy of hers.

She said:

"Well, Nevis, I hear that you're making Simon take you to Venice. What a treat that will be for you! You mustn't miss the Bellinis."

And as though the memory of that benignly-curving maternity had started a train of thought, she looked approvingly at Gwen's jabot, less approvingly at the faint curves that swelled my printed dress. I made up my mind to miss the Bellinis.

In five minutes Colin was howling; the nurse's pleasant face was red and resentful; nervous atmospheric vibrations seemed to beat against the walls. All unconscious, Mrs. Quinn said crisply:

"Dear, dear, what a naughty little boy! I don't believe you're firm enough with him, Gwen. Adrian had such a temper at that age."

The child howled louder. Gwen said nervously:

"Let's go and have tea."

The green drawing-room was cool and pleasant. The sun-blinds were drawn; there were masses fresh carnations, apricot and mauve and striped like glass marbles. The cucumber-sandwiches were paper-thin. Gwen's parlourmaid was neater than Katie.

"Delightful!" said Mrs. Quinn. "Isn't it delightful, Nevis?"

The very way that she bit into a cucumber-sandwich was a reproach. See this delightful room, it said; this young woman in an interesting and delightful situation. Go thou and do likewise! With one strong gulp she drained her tea-cup and set it firmly down. I wondered if she would have liked Gwen's remark about a sack of potatoes. No; motherhood had to be something refined and idealised, like a Bellini Madonna who could have given birth to nothing more earthly than a butterfly. Her mind was a kind of filter through which everything passed and came out desperately refined. If you died you were said to have "passed away;" if you were going to have a baby you were put through the filter and came out "about to reproduce." Mrs. Quinn's filtered version of life made it seem a singularly bloodless affair.

The bamboos rustled dryly and incessantly, the brisk voice talked on and on. I began to be oppressed by the familiar sensations of suffocation and despair that, battering against Colin's baby consciousness, had found outlet in a roar. But I could not roar. Even that relief was denied me. Gwen's colour, seen full in the light, was quite ghastly.

"Off already, Nevis? Such an elusive person—we never seem to see her, do we, Gwen?"

"I'll come and see you off, Nevis. Two minutes, dear, and I'll be back."

At the door I whispered fiercely:

"Don't let that wretched woman tire you out. She's an absolute vampire."

"Oh, I don't know. She means awfully well, you know."

"Oh, Gwen, your damnable, damnable sweetness! It will kill you one of these days."

"Don't be an idiot."

I had gone down two steps of the stairs, and I looked back. She was standing smiling, with her hand on the door. There was pathos in that child's head covered in short, waving fair hair, the contradiction of that slow-moving, mature body and those empty blue eyes. If Gwen lived to be a hundred she would still remain curiously remote from life. She had known passion and given birth, yet the experiences had left her untouched. I could picture her as an old woman with just the same white skin, just the same innocent clarity of expression. Gwen would never grow old because all the violent emotions knew her not.

And something made me say:

"When I get back we must see more of each other, Gwen. I don't see enough of you."

"Well, you can't help that. You're always busy."

"Oh, I can find time. You'll want a lot of new clothes after the baby. If I'm not too hard up, we might go over to Paris and have an orgy."

"Would you?" She looked pleased and grateful. "That would be lovely, Nevis. Have a good time in Venice."

"Take care of yourself, my dear."

"I will."

She smiled and waved her hand. The door shut. I went quickly downstairs, feeling depressed. Hollow mechanical noises floated up from the lift shaft; someone rattled the gates in the vestibule and a moment later was wafted past me. It was Adrian, standing very erect in the little lighted box, his long, sensitive face tilted upwards with a sickeningly smug expression, as though he were an ascending apostle hoping to find God on the top floor. He did not see me running swiftly down the dark spiral staircase. I thought "Poor Gwen." She would sit, gentle and kind, between the two of them. They would turn their tall bodies and their sharp, high noses towards her; they would quack, quack incessantly in the same dry voice, and the vibrations of their common nervousness would batter against the walls. Both Adrian and his mother were terribly nervous; their nervousness was something hot and fretful that sucked the vitality out of the atmosphere like blotting-paper. Adrian was a fretter. At the sight of something not quite right—a plate not quite hot enough, or a riding-boot not quite polished—his lips would lift back in a grimace of distaste, and his nostrils would dilate in the snuffle of a bad-tempered horse who has been offered a rotten carrot. But he would say nothing. To lose the temper publicly was "bad form."

Yes, Gwen would sit between the two of them, and instead of saying "For God's sake shut up!" she would continue to answer gently and kindly. Yes, Mrs. Quinn. No, Mrs. Quinn. Yes, Adrian darling. No, Adrian darling. Afterwards, perhaps, she would go and lie down in a darkened room and say, "I have just a little headache, but you mustn't wait dinner for me, Adrian darling." Oh, damn everything!

I went out into the street. It was after six o'clock, and the slanting light was rich and heavy. No one was about except a white Persian cat who sat on a gate-post and stared with pale-blue eyes across the square. Pale-blue eyes like Gwen's. I looked about me as I walked. These big houses, amongst which was the block of flats where Gwen lived, had not the emaciated elegance of the houses in a Paris *Place*; they had no romance, no grace, but only a sort of solid dignity and, with most of their windows shuttered, mystery. Life was full of mysteries. I thought again of Gwen, and I thought, "I don't really know her. I'll never know her." All round me in these houses, living their secret, tantalising lives, were people whom I did not know and whom I would never know. And yet, my God, I try to write books. All the people, the places, the colour and excitement and life in the world, and I shall miss them. Waste, waste, waste! I shall die without knowing two things about the lives of a native in Central Africa, or a ventriloquist or a Cambridge professor. The awful waste and pathos of life; everyone shut up in themselves, shuttered like these houses; trying to let in strangers and failing; carrying their secrets with them to the grave.

I felt suddenly tired and dejected. I thought, "I hate summer," and my mind went forward gladly to autumn. After our holiday I would come back refreshed, eager for work; in the week-ends we would go into the country. I thought of riding on the Downs in keen, bitter air; of yellow leaves lying thick in the shadow of a privet hedge; of chilly mists creeping closely, jealously over the sparkling ground, and bare branches making such a miraculous dark weaving that one cried out in silent ecstasy: "Ah, do not bud again! Keep away, spring!" Simon would laugh and be happy. I would laugh and be happy. And we would come back in the evenings, contented enough to feel the stuffy, companionable brightness of a town; to stretch out our muddy riding-boots towards the fire and eat hot crumpets and dream. I must read a lot this autumn and hear some music. ... Hell, how tired I am!

"Taxi!"

I put my key in the blue front door. The little hall smelt of fried plaice. Simon's bowler hat lay on the table and his voice demanded angrily out of the sitting-room:

"Where the hell have you been?"

He was in a bad temper because Roddy Talent had dropped in for a drink and had only just gone. He mimicked savagely: "My dear, I do love your *house*. I think all those mirrors are *quite terribly* clever. Nevis is so marvellous at all that sort of *thing*, isn't she?" And he added: "My God!"

"He's not bad really, you know, Simon. Affected, of course, but awfully sensitive and rather pathetic. I hope you weren't too rude to him."

"Pathetic hell," said Simon. "Where have you been, anyway?"

But suddenly he emerged from his bad temper and became very gay and mad dog. He said:

"By God, only another two days and we'll be off. Realise that, Nevis? Let's have a drink."

We had several drinks, and became exhilarated and introspective. All through dinner I talked happily of Shelley and Simon did not listen, while Simon talked happily of stag-hunting and I did not listen. This is the only sensible way of conducting a conversation. After dinner we decided that we must go off at once and see someone, so we went round to the Kirkpatricks and played noisy bridge until one in the morning. Then Simon said expansively to Peter Kirkpatrick:

"That's the worst of these women, Peter. They don't realise that we have to punch the clock at nine every morning. Thanks, I'll have another whisky."

Life did not seem a mystery any more. On the contrary, it seemed extremely friendly and safe, and a little, a very little, unsteady. We drove home, and the night was magical. There were enormous stars, surely several times larger than on other nights. I lay back in the car, languid, musing, looking up at them.

> To love and bear; to hope till hope creates
> From its own wreck the thing it contemplates;
> Neither to change nor falter nor repent. ...

Something sonorous and deep and clanging about that, like a trumpet blowing out of the Old Testament. A bleak cathedral shape against the sky. Difficult beauty; painful, almost; but beauty ought to be difficult and painful and too deep for words. *Neither to change nor falter nor repent.* Ah, that was good!

> This, like thy glory, Titan, is to be
> Great, good and joyous, beautiful and free!
> This is alone Life, Joy, Empire and Victory.

"Oh, Simon, Shelley is ... Shelley is so ..."

❧

In another week we would be in Venice.

VIII

Harvest ran before us, yellow torch in hand, all the way from Strasbourg through the Black Forest to the Engadine. The land was sleek and fat as a young heifer; emerald pastures so brilliant that they looked freshly watered; rustling corn and barley bent in strange arabesques by a hot wind. Branches clotted with small red apples and pears leant down into the dusty road. Everywhere we heard the clatter of reaper and threshing-machine; the groan of carts laden with broad leaves of maize and yellow swedes. The plodding cream-coloured oxen shook their heads in a cloud of flies. "Ai!" shouted the young men. "Ai! Ai! Ai!" and they jerked forward. A turnip fell in the road. The wheels passed over it and pulped it into the white dust.

I lay back half asleep. My hat was on the floor and the wind was in my hair; my face and arms burned. In these valleys there was such an indescribable, a suffocating atmosphere of sunshine and sweat and warm earth; they were like the armpits of a great, genial god. The air was yeasty with harvest. I felt drugged and stupid, nauseated and at peace. I tried to think of Cora and Marcus and Mrs. Quinn. I thought "The Brompton Road is still there," and it seemed wildly improbable. Nothing was real, nothing had shape or substance but these straining oxen, these sweating men, these fields that slipped from gold to emerald, from wine-colour and russet back to gold.

Although it was Sunday they were still working quietly and

doggedly; men, women and children, stooping and straining in the afternoon sun. The women wore cotton bodices and striped aprons. The men were naked to the waist and burnt a deep red-brown; on their chests were golden hairs and drops of sweat glistened among the hairs. They were like splendid animals. It was wonderful to see them stoop and swing a load of maize aloft as though it were a flower. No doubt they could not sign their own names, and a powerful animal smell came from their bodies, but they moved against the rich fields like figures in some noble frieze of toil. The older men seemed to lose that physical quality; their bodies were shrivelled and blackened with sun; in the shadow of their broad plaited hats their faces were seamed with a thousand lines and their eyes blinked redly like the eyes of an old dog. But "Ai! Ai! Ai-ee!" shouted the young men, and the hairs on their great chests glistened.

We got out of the car and ate our lunch under some apple-trees. A million insects hummed among the harebells. Simon lay flat on his back, smoking a cigarette. He was hatless; the sun had bleached his hair to a bright gold.

"Why do we move on? Let's stay here. I like this place."

"So do I. But wait until you see Venice."

"I like these people." From the road came a shrill "Ai! Ai!" and the crack of a whip. The dust rose in languid white pillars. "My God! they're lucky. They live up here. They don't putrefy slowly in a stinking office."

"But it's too sensuous, too purely physical. It's like a creeping sort of chloroform. Lovely but lethal! If we lived here I'd never do any work."

"Who the hell wants to work?" asked Simon.

It seemed quite unanswerable.

We went on. Green spirals of hops leant inwards like

wigwams. The cottage gardens overflowed with hot coloured flowers that seemed to prey upon each other, to writhe in steaming contortions of perfume and colour. Each hollyhock was taller than the last; crimson convolvulus stretched out fibrous arms and choked sunflowers that stood as high as Prussian Guards. A cock scrambled up on a wall, leaving his wives to scratch among the dung, and crowed hoarsely, "Cock-a-doodle-doo! I am a male!" His red comb swelled. Satisfied, he went jauntily back to the dung.

It was a curiously male country; strong, a little coarse; warm and virile. Orchards, corn, children and bantams among the dung, flowers, the plod of oxen, the golden hairs on the chests of the young men. But the patient earth was female; these valleys its vast child-bed; the groan of laden carts its labour cries. One could almost see it open and contract in one titanic, suffering effort to spew out the grain and the red fruit and the roots that were buried deep in its body.

"I'd like a child some time, Simon."

He gave me a quick, strange look.

"So should I."

And I knew somehow that he wanted a child badly and had never said anything about it. He asked, not looking at me:

"Now?"

"I'm not sure. Are you?"

"No. In some ways I want a child like hell, and in others I'm afraid of it."

"That's how I feel. But suddenly I felt … I don't know. We may be missing something. Let's start one when we get back to England."

Simon laughed.

"Why are you laughing?"

"Let's wait until we get back to England and see how you feel then."

"I don't see why you're laughing, Simon."

That night we stopped at a funny little *Gasthaus* among the pines. The walls and floor were plain varnished pine; two stout German climbers sat playing draughts beside a huge green china stove. The water in the bedroom pitcher was ice-cold, and from two inadequate little wooden hangers billowed two vast balloons of feather eiderdowns. Somehow or other we managed to sleep in one of the hangers, locked in each other's arms. There was no room to turn either way, and the balloon showed distressing tendencies to float off into a larger Beyond. But all night the sound of cow-bells came down the hillside, crystal sounds dropping into the crystal quiet. It was a night like no other night. There was no desire about it, only a quiet, safe happiness. The little room smelt of pines; it was cold with the austere coldness of a glacier stream. I thought strangely: "You will never be so happy again."

Dawn and my cramped body woke me. Simon was lying with his arms flung out. Sleep gave his face a queer milk-white pallor; his pyjama jacket was open and the red-gold hairs shone on the white chest. I thought of the young men urging on the bullocks: "Ai! Ai! Ai-ee!" He was breathing very quietly. I watched him for a few minutes, full of confused, half-sad thoughts, before slipping cautiously out of the curve of his body and getting into the other bed.

The next day we began to climb higher. The pine forests became more dense; the short grass was carpeted with white and yellow woodruff, campion in withered bladders, small purple harebells and scabious. It was still hot, but not with the suffocating, sensuous heat of the valleys. The air was crisp, with a tang that came straight off cold, absinthe-coloured torrents and high pockets of snow.

I felt full of sudden energy. For three days my brain had been a hot, dormant thing, preoccupied with sunburn and gnat-bites and my next meal. Now I began to talk more briskly and to wish that I had brought my work. The Brompton Road became probable once more. We bought peaches from the little *coiffeur* in the village and looked up the steep tracks that climb like children into the laps of the mountains. I wanted to go at them all in a run.

But the foot-hills were pleasant. We sat in the grass, looking down at a little island, conical with pine trees, that rose from the middle of a pale blue lake. Grasshoppers bounded about us, making an endless racket; giant fellows with green heads and hard, shiny bodies that looked as though they had been cut out of painted tin. Scraping their athletic thighs together, they made fabulous leaps over the white mountain thistles.

"About having a child, Simon. I've been thinking. We don't want one yet."

"No."

"We couldn't possibly afford it, darling."

"No."

I heaved a relieved sigh. If you looked like poor Gwen was looking you could not run down a mountain path. You could not lie on your flat little belly watching a small snake wriggle on his flat little belly over the pine-needles. Decidedly preferable to be oneself, sprawling in the hot sun and the smell of wet mosses. Simon was laughing. Why are you laughing, Simon? But I did not much care.

"I wish we weren't going back to London."

"God! I should think so."

"All our quarrels are about other people. I've said that before, but it's so damnably, profoundly true. When we get away by ourselves like this we're quite different, Simon."

"And the moment we get back Marcus Chard will telephone, Oonagh will telephone, Roddy will come round and ask you to a perfectly divine show of bloody little Russian tea-cosies. … Don't laugh, damn you. It will all start over again. Won't it?"

"Yes."

"Then what's the use of talking?"

"I don't know," I said in a depressed voice.

The tip of the snake's tail vanished with a derisive wiggle among the ferns. Simon said slowly:

"The trouble is, we love each other but we're so damn egotistical. I hate giving in, and so do you."

I didn't want to be serious. I wanted to look back in a mood of easy sentimentality and remember only the times when we had been happy and laughed together; not all those times when I had felt like packing a bag and slamming the blue front door so hard that they would hear me in Ennismore Gardens. So I said the first coarse thing that came into my head, and Simon laughed. He picked me out of the moss and we went down the little path to lunch.

So, at last, to Verona, where we left the car. The hot train and the small white grapes that Simon bought for me; the English lady in the Henry Heath felt hat sitting opposite, waving a Japanese paper fan. Over her head was the sad beauty of Giorgione's most perfect picture: the mother suckling her child, the young man watching, and round them both the mysterious blue and green gloom; the feeling of doom and suspense that waits to be broken by the first roll of thunder. The lady in the Henry Heath felt hat, after one glance, had averted her eyes. "What a thing to put in a railway-carriage!" Her chest was virtuously flat; her lean thighs would scrape against each other as she walked with the desiccated sound of locknit against locknit. Directoire knickers, S.W., 6/11d. at Derry & Tom's. How Giorgione could paint naked flesh! The curtain of heavy rep, drawn against the sun, flapped dustily in my face. ...

Until at last "Venezia! Venezia! Venezia!" and a genial, black-bearded ruffian of a *faccino* leapt into the carriage, wresting the suitcases from our hands.

Four days later a shadow fell across my face as I lay on the scorching sands of the Lido, and, looking up, I saw Marcus Chard.

IX

ૐ

We had spent every day at the Lido, but not on the Excelsior beach. Simon said: "When I want to see American peeresses getting tight on champagne cocktails I can go to the Embassy." So we jolted along in a tram through the broad, tree-lined streets to the Stabilimento Bagni, where all the Venetians go with their bathing-dresses in neat little newspaper parcels under their arms. A stout woman tried to sell us an American sailor hat and beads and some very ugly shawls.

When I stripped I felt disgustingly white and unhealthy, like some queer fungus grown in a cellar. All the Venetians were so brown, especially the men. Their bodies were astonishingly beautiful, polished to the sleekness of golden marble, and they walked proudly, like gods. In the water they were glistening brown fishes, agile and laughing. And they looked at me with a slow, appraising stare that peeled the *maillot* off my back and left me naked. Some of them even spoke to me in soft, laughing Italian, and were not a whit disconcerted when I answered back in polite French.

The young women were beautiful too. I said disconsolately to Simon: "I wish I had a bit more bosom," for their bosoms were almost impertinently rounded, and they moved as though the hot sands were the red carpet of kings. None of your scuttling Anglo-Saxon modesty about it, either. Breasts well out, haunches swaying, they walked like lionesses padding along in their native jungle, and lay purring on the sands while their lovely brown children snarled over their bodies.

I said to Simon that the whole of the Lido was rather like a jungle: the blazing heat; the stench of animalism, of thousands of panting, sweating bodies; the sleek young breasts and haunches. Even the water was warm, and green as an aquamarine. I floated in it languidly, half asleep. Simon swam far out, beyond the scatter of boats and bathers; soon his head was a dark cork bobbing against the froth of incoming waves. I lay on the sand with closed eyes and thought how strange it was that one's whole life should be bound up with an anonymous dark cork bobbing about among a lot of other anonymous corks. I lay in a hot doze, conscious of a duet of excited Italian voices near me; of the sunburn on my back; of a shadow that fell across my face and did not move. I looked up.

"Marcus!"

For a moment he made no answering sign of recognition. He loomed darkly over me, a thick, compact figure blocking out the sun. I shaded my eyes with one hand and stared stupidly up at him.

"It is you, isn't it?"

And laughing, stammering a lot of disjointed questions, I reached out and caught hold of his hands.

"But how? And where from? And why didn't you? … I'm so glad to see you! Sit down."

"I rang you up from Paris and they said you'd gone to Venice. I thought 'That's a pretty swell idea'—Paris was hot as hell—so I got on the first train and went straight to Danieli's. The hall-porter told me you bathed from the Stabilimento Bagni." He laughed, and looked me up and down. "Well, how are you after all that? My God, you're looking fine."

"Wait till you see Simon—he's out there somewhere, swimming. Marcus, you brute, I can't tell you how pleased I am to see you. Why did you disappear like that?"

He said shortly: "I had to see someone in Paris. ... By the way, I'm going back on the *Bremen* in ten days."

"For good?"

"I'm afraid so."

"Damn it, Marcus, how am I going to get on without you? Don't laugh. I mean it."

He looked out towards the bathers for a minute. Three fishing-boats had appeared, sailing slowly from the direction of Venice; one with burnt terra-cotta sails; the others a clear pure yellow like brimstone butterflies. They seemed to float between glassy sea and glassy sky, light aerial things, without substance.

"Why not come too?"

I smiled uncertainly. He still looked out at the red and yellow sails.

"If only I could!"

"Well, why not?" he repeated. He faced me suddenly and disconcertingly, eyes very bright under those thick brows that were peppered with white hairs.

"Are you serious?"

"Surely!"

While I hesitated, Simon came over the sands towards us. In four days he had got nearly as brown as the Venetians; he was naked to the waist, and his skin shone as though it had been oiled. I thought helplessly how beautiful he was. He was looking with a fascinated expression at a stout German who was lying asleep with a red handkerchief over his head, belly pulsing up and down like some flabby marine obscenity. Then he caught sight of Marcus.

It struck me that he did not look very surprised. He came up to us easily and held out a hand.

"Hallo, Chard!"

As they talked I seemed to fall into the role of silent onlooker. I lay back again and watched them through half-shut lids. And since on this beach one thought in terms of the physical, it was Simon who seemed to dominate the situation. Simon, with his beautiful straight back and his strong legs; his wet hair was a bright greenish-gold. He laughed suddenly, and his teeth were silk-white against the tanned skin. I despised myself for the pleasure with which I watched him. I despised myself for thinking that Marcus, in his careful English suit, looked thick and clumsy; that his hands were too carefully manicured, and that in five more years he would have a paunch. He was looking at me. I said confusedly:

"What did you say?"

"I asked how you were liking this."

"The Lido?"

"No, my God, this lion-house! You can smell the sawdust and the raw meat. I mean Venice."

"Venice!" I laughed and looked at Simon. "We take the steamer out here every morning and here we stay all day. In the evening we have coffee and *fines* at Florian's. That's all of Venice I've seen."

"But that's disgraceful!" He looked really shocked. "You see, I know it rather well. I was here for several months in 1914. You'll have to let me show you round."

Simon said sleepily: "I'm glad you've turned up, Chard. Nevis was finding me damn boring. Well, I'm going to dress."

"And then you must dine with me. Do you know the Bonvecchiati? It might amuse you to look in at the opera afterwards. They're probably giving *Rigoletto*—excruciatingly bad and delightfully in earnest."

But they were giving *Butterfly*, and Pinkerton was in full swing when we arrived, for we had sat too long under the vines at the Bonvecchiati. I had eaten a prodigious quantity of *scampi*, and talked too much; Marcus always roused in me a wild desire to show off. The two men had laughed and applauded, and I had felt a little light-headed with excitement, conscious that a chain of jagged corals looked well against my white dress and sunburnt skin and that a young Italian was giving me amorous glances over his tooth-pick.

I felt that it was very amusing to be watching Marcus and Simon together. It was exciting, like something in a play, and I had to suppress a desire to laugh very loudly. Now that Simon was clothed in a dinner-jacket they seemed to meet on equal terms, shirt-front for shirt-front. The beautiful young savage of the Lido had vanished; it was Marcus who was the dominant figure here, ordering dinner in quick, decisive Italian, and being the most delightful of companions. I glanced triumphantly from him to Simon.

"Simon, hasn't Marcus got a wonderful head?"

"Wonderful head," Simon repeated impressively, nodding several times.

The young Italian made a cradle of his hands and scavenged his wisdom-tooth with a serious spiritual expression. His black eyes rolled towards me. I burst out laughing. It was only when I stepped into a gondola and the lights blurred pleasantly, the silver prow cut through the solid blue dusk as though it were cheese, that I realised how tight I was.

The little opera-house was stiflingly hot. There were very few English and no one was dressed. Madame Butterfly was toddling among a chorus of middle-aged geishas, whose tired, anxious faces looked pathetic under the puffed wigs and the cherry flowers. But they toddled, they flirted their idiotic fans, they essayed a rather ghastly imitation of girlish laughter. I leant over to Marcus and said in a hissing whisper, "I'm tight!"

The beauty, the inevitable, hackneyed beauty of the duet sobered me. I listened, and tears came into my eyes. Butterfly, bursting out of her obi, was carrying my soul on a pure top A up to God. In vain I told myself that this was water-and-grenadine, the easiest and most debased form of taking music. The tears stung my eyes, and turning to Marcus so that he could get a good view of them, I said, "I'm so happy, Marcus!" It seemed to me that it was wonderful to be sitting there between Simon and Marcus, all of us happy, listening to music. In his stall Simon slept, bolt upright. Suddenly he woke up and applauded violently.

Interval, more music, more interval. The curtains parted silently on that lovely, mysterious beginning of the last act, the immobile figure against the dawn, the stage strewn with branches of cherry-blossom. Quiet music, a mere thread of sound. And on it my mind began to play strange gymnastics. I thought of the new book for the first time since I had left England, the new, unwritten book that was to be about Simon, Gwen and Adrian, Cora, myself, Mrs. Quinn. ... But suddenly I knew that we were going to be shadowy figures in the background, and that the whole book was Simon, my husband Simon. His personality emerged, dominant, as this theme was emerging from the music. I thought of him on the lawn at Red Court; his light eyes and dusty gold hair, and my feeling that he was going to barge ruthlessly into the nice, tidy little pattern of my life. He stirred beside me, and his shirt-front creaked.

On the other side Marcus leant forward, his expression a little sardonic, a clump of thick dark hair hanging down his forehead. In the darkness his eyes met mine. I had a disquieting feeling that he could read my thoughts.

A knife hurtled from behind a screen and clattered on the boards. There was the thud of a falling body. Poor Butterfly was lying there, stout and pleased with herself, thinking of the baby octopus that she was going to eat for supper.

꙳

"Do you know, Marcus, I'm getting to be one of those tiresome people who can only enjoy things in retrospect. All this"—I pointed to the lagoons and the fishing-boats—"will be much more real and beautiful to me when I'm sitting in a cinema in Leicester Square. Yet I remember motoring down to Devonshire when I was fifteen, and everything was piercingly real. I soaked up impressions. My first pink sheep was far more of a genuine experience than my first Giorgione."

We were in a gondola, coming away from Torcello. We had been rowed up the tiny waterway, hedged with pink and mauve river-herbs, to the vast, lonely cathedral that springs out of the weeds, and it had left me with a strange feeling of depression. It was inhuman as a pile of bones bleaching in the sun. I thought of the vulgar, laughing workmen of the sixth century who had swarmed about these walls and drunk their wine in the sheds and spat cheerfully on the ground. They had gone, but their loving handiwork remained. Poor, sad ghost, it could not die. On the wall mosaic sinners writhed in mosaic flames and were prodded back again by unpleasant angels when they attempted to crawl out, but there was no one there to impress. The whole thing was apologetic, like a trick that was once good and now fails to come off.

Marcus had made no comment on my plaintive comparison of pink sheep and Giorgiones. I said impatiently: "Well, what do you think it is? Old age?"

But instead of answering, he asked slowly:

"Do you know what I think you'd better do?"

"What?"

"Come to New York."

I stared at him, and laughed.

"I thought you were joking the other day on the Lido."

"I told you I wasn't."

"Yes, but—you forget that I've got a husband and a house and two rather incompetent servants. Not to mention work—"

"That's what I mean. Work! Come for three or four months and settle down to that novel of yours. I believe that you'd do the best work of your life there."

"If only I could!"

"Why not?" He looked at me impatiently. "What's keeping you?"

"Simon, for one thing."

He shrugged his shoulders as though he did not care for the reason.

"Three months isn't very long. But I think that it would be long enough to get you a brand-new set of contacts and ideas. We can't risk you forgetting all about *The Forcing House* and becoming just a nice young English matron with a baby-carriage and a Morris-Oxford car.

I burst into helpless laughter.

"What a nasty fate, Marcus! I didn't know you could be so spiteful."

But he remained grim.

"Why don't you come over this fall? I'm serious."

"Because, my dear, it's wildly impossible."

He was silent. I repeated: "Wildly impossible! For one thing, there's the question of bank-balances. New York isn't cheap, they tell me."

"Well"—he hesitated—"I have an idea."

"You have?" I twisted round so that I could watch his face. But he said unexpectedly:

"Has it ever struck you that you are a very incurious young woman? You have never tried to find out if I have ever committed murder, been a bootlegger, married—"

"Are you married?"

"I had to go to Paris so suddenly the other day to see my wife. She is over here to get a divorce."

He spoke briskly. Two fishing-boats passed us. One had brown sails on which was painted a crude Virgin and Child; the other was decorated with an inscrutable blue-and-yellow eye. I stared at it, and wondered what sort of a woman had married Marcus Chard.

"That being so, I don't suppose that I shall have much more use for our apartment. Rosalind furnished it—I never cared about it, anyway. But there's a pretty big studio, which was what decided me to take the place."

He was silent, thinking. I wondered how Rosalind had furnished it; there is so much character in furniture. I decided that it would be careful period Italian, breaking out in an occasional rash of cherry-coloured vestments and headless saints. All done with a religious regard to detail, and even the lavatory plugs disguised as something chaste in Florentine wrought-iron, the telephone doing its best to look like a sixteenth-century sacramental ark. … Suddenly I had a very, clear picture of the upper part of Rosalind's face: Alpine-blue eyes under a clever forehead, the bridge of a delicate, decisive nose. And how they would quarrel, those two, among their sacramental arks and interior decorator's tomfoolery!

"If you come to New York, and care to use it, there it is. That's a big item gone off your budget. Rents are pretty high, and you couldn't work in an hotel."

"But what about you?"

"I should live at my club for a bit. Don't worry! I hate the place. I'll get rid of it, anyway, but if you can make use of it first—"

"For three months?"

"Three months—three years—what does it matter? Good God, child!"—he looked at me furiously—"here is the big chance that will make you, and you don't jump to it! What's the matter with you?"

"I don't know. Don't be cross with me."

"I'm not cross with you." He laughed, and back came the benevolent wrinkles.

"Why are you so kind to me? That's what I want to know."

"Kind!" he jeered. "Are you kidding yourself that this is just idle philanthropy? My dear, innocent child! You're an author, I'm a publisher. I'm seeing myself in the rôle of fosterer of youthful genius. Guide, philosopher and friend, you know, with a three-books contract tucked up the sleeve."

"You make me nervous. Supposing I fail?"

"You won't fail."

"Promise?" I laughed uncertainly. "Promise that if I come to New York?—"

"San Francesco in Deserto, signori!" called the gondolier.

"Marcus, I'm a fool. It's quite impossible. Quite. You've no idea of the opposition that everyone would raise."

"Do you really care about opposition?"

I felt like bursting into tears.

"Later on—next year, perhaps—"

He got up and held out his hand.

"Come along. Let's go and look at the little monastery."

His face was quite inscrutable, the full lips pursed together, the heavy eyelids drooping. I walked unhappily down the cool, whitewashed cloisters beside him. A young lay-brother with glasses and bright, friendly blue eyes showed us the chapel, where an older monk was mending a fused wire. Happy and absorbed as a small child, he hardly glanced up at our entrance. The young lay-brother said something to Marcus and glanced at me.

"What does he say?"

"There is one part of the monastery where women are not allowed to go—the sleeping-quarters, probably."

"All right; I'll wait here."

I sat down on the edge of a brick wall. The sunshine was hot on my shoulders. What utter quiet! Torcello with its dead cathedral, and now this island, where men live who are already dead. I thought suddenly and with passionate longing of Simon. How wise to stay on the Lido with its reassuring animal smells, its swaying haunches, its lovely, unashamed sensuality! A bell tolled. A small, bright insect ran over the mosses on the wall; hesitated before a crevice; hurried on.

The little courtyard was surrounded by windows. I glanced up, and on the sill immediately over me was a pair of old boots. They were shabby things, white with dust and cracked across both toes. Someone had taken them off his poor, hot, aching feet and put them out to cool. I looked at them, and suddenly I knew the simplicity and the frugal, uncomplaining meekness of these lives. Those boots were pathetic and ludicrous. They convinced one of the existence of God, and they made one think of tender, throbbing bunions. ... I laughed out loud. My heart was suddenly quiet. The boots said, "New York? What does it matter? What does anything matter?" There was the sound of subdued singing. The bearded monk was humming a chant, as happily, bending his short-sighted eyes close to the task, he mended a fuse to the glory of God.

Marcus and the young lay-brother came through the cloisters. The young lay-brother was talking volubly, ingenuously pleased to have a listener. We walked back to the gondola. Marcus looked at his watch.

"Time for one Bellini before we go over to the Lido to pick up Simon. No, I insist! Ah, it's such a lovely thing. Why are you laughing?"

"My mother-in-law told me that I mustn't miss the Bellinis."

"She was perfectly right."

"Yes," I said meekly.

But it was strange that as we stood in the sacristy of the Frari, in front of Bellini's triptych, the Madonna reminded me a little of Gwen. I remembered that later. Gwen's face, as I had seen it last against the green walls of her drawing-room, was more fragile and colourless, but the expression of the brow was strangely like, and just for a moment I felt a pang of anxiety. I thought, "That wretched business—I wish it were over," and then the rich blues and greens of the pictures soaked into my eyes and I forgot her.

Marcus dropped me at Danieli's and went off to fetch Simon from the Lido. He said we might all dine at some new place in the Giardini. I went slowly through the cool entrance-hall and upstairs by lift. Our room overlooked a wide canal where gondoliers quarrelled and joked and spat all day. The ceiling, from which hung a hideous monstrosity in blown glass, was bright with sliding, curdling reflections of water.

On the table was a new pad of writing-paper that I had bought from a shop at the corner of the Piazza. My brain was teeming with thoughts. Into it slid the music of *Butterfly*, and quietly, so mingled with the mounting cadences of the 'cellos that it was indistinguishable from them, the opening lines of my new book. Quietly, almost furtively, I drew the pad towards me and wrote "Chapter I." Quietly, almost furtively …

"Knock!"

Everything fell to pieces. Down in the alley a raucous voice shouted something vile. And the heat was awful, like an oven.

"Yes? Come in! *Entrate!*"

A white-uniformed lift-boy came in with a telegram.

"Poor little Gwen died last night giving birth prematurely to beautiful girl terrible grief to us all should like you home mother." The something vile was answered by a second voice from over the water, but that sounded more good-natured and there was a bellow of laughter. An American voice called next door: "Oh, Emily! What did you do with my Harper's Bazaar, dear?"

"No answer."

Absolutely no answer. I sat down heavily and stared at the stupid pattern of my writing on the white page.

X

꙼

We left for Verona that evening; Marcus said that he would follow us next day. He was extraordinarily kind and helpful, getting the tickets, seeing to the luggage, and wiring the garage to have the car ready. As the train crawled out of the station I looked out, and there he was, a short, sturdy figure, waving a black felt hat. It reminded me of our first lunch together: the bright courtyard, and Marcus standing immobile among the wardrobe trunks. By a queer coincidence we were in a carriage with another reproduction of the famous Giorgione. It seemed inexpressibly sad; I thought that I would never be able to look at its mysterious blurred greens and thundery blues again without feeling a sensation of shock and horror.

We took it in turns to drive. I should not have minded driving all the time, for having something to do took my mind off Gwen. It was worse having to sit still, watching the road creep ahead into the gorge of the mountains; watching the character of the land change and, presently, the poplars slide by in a dream; and thinking, endlessly thinking.

It was strange what an effect Gwen's death had on my nerves. I had been fond of her, but not very fond. We were like two people stranded on separate islands, unable to converse except by amiable signals. She was so typical of her kind: the smart brigade of Pont Street girls with their silver-fox scarves and their bridge; their fairly good French; their alert patter of the new books and plays; their complete, devastating absence of any sort of mental life. Gwen would pipe up her piece about the last Huxley or the show of Epstein's so brightly, but that very brightness rang false. It was the mechanical brightness of the pianola, the hollow, repertory brightness of the parrot who shrieks "Good-morning, good-morning! 'Allo! 'Allo!"

Yet her death shocked me horribly. I kept on saying to myself, "Gwen, of all people!" Gwen, who had not a base thought in her head, and she had been allowed to die in such pain. She must have died in pain. Mrs. Quinn would tell me that the end was peaceful, and everything possible had been done, but she had died in twisting, sweating, inhuman pain. I knew. Bellini's conception of maternity as something benign and gentle was false. The dignity and pathos of those boots on the monastery window-sill were false. Everything was false and ugly; there was no escape. Monstrous outrages like the murder of Gwen were allowed to happen, and yet every moment, all round us, men and women were struggling to remain in such a world. They were trying in their millions to cling to life instead of loosening their grip and sinking back into the quiet stream.

I sat staring ahead in a dark abyss of misery. I had not known such misery when Mother and Father had died. Yes, once before, when my cousin David had been killed in a motor accident. What misery! I was fourteen at the time, and we had been going to marry and live in a Tudor mansion that we had seen illustrated in *Country Life*, and our two children were to be called Robert and Margaret. Why Robert and Margaret? I had forgotten. But I remembered weeping in an agony of rage at the injustice of David dying with his beautiful white body smashed into a pulp.

Only David and Gwen had meant that to me. What had they

got in common? Youth? The appalling, criminal unexpectedness of the thing? My mother had been ill so long that the process was gradual, the misery more drawn out, but there had been time to get used to the idea. When my father's horse overturned in a ditch everyone seemed to be especially kind to me, and I was left with the confused impression that death was rather exciting like a holiday, with new clothes and sherry all round. Only David and Gwen. ...

There was a stiff breeze in the Channel, and I hoped fervently that I would be sick. Anything to stop thinking. Anything to get rid of that bruised, heavy feeling round the heart and transfer it to the reassuring region of the stomach.

> Do I forget? Retchings twist and tie me. ...
> Do I remember? Acrid return and slimy,
> The sobs and slobbers of a last year's woe.

When I was fifteen I was in love with Rupert Brooke. Gwen, of all people. ... Gwen, of *all* people. ...

Simon said: "Do you feel bad?"

"Yes. I'm going down."

I looked at him with sudden cold disdain. His light eyes and narrow head reminded me for a minute of Adrian, and it was through Adrian that Gwen had ceased to think and feel and be. The Quinns were a crushing force; sooner or later one gave up struggling. It did not really matter whether the death was bodily or spiritual. The result was the same. One ceased to be as a separate entity. The Quinns came out on top; the angels of Prince's Gate triumphed over the angels of Parnassus. ...

"Excuse me. Oh, I'm so sorry. Excuse me."

The damn boat was lurching, and I lurched too,

companionably. I wished that the crossing would prolong itself into hours, years. Downstairs it was quiet, peopled with the ghosts of old meals and eau de cologne, full of strange sounds that took one's mind off everything but the disgusting possibilities of the human race. Upstairs there was Simon, the approaching shape of England, the advancing spirit of the Quinns.

⋇

"What a crossing! Really dreadful for the time of year. ... Porter! I thought I'd better keep it in its band-box, just as it came from the shop. Excuse me. Porter! Oh, excuse me. *Goodbye*, I *do* hope we all meet again at Cadenabbia next year. Such a jolly party. *Porter, where are you taking those golf clubs?*"

"How do you feel, Nevis?"

"All right."

The correct answer is, "Nothing at all."

Absolutely numb from the waist up.

Montpelier Place was looking dusty and unattractive. The maids were away and I had forgotten to wire for them. Even James was at kennels in the country. The house was in the hands of a policeman's widow who shuffled about in carpet slippers and lurked like a whelk in the basement with a very old, bloated terrier bitch. The policeman's widow said that she would run round the corner for a bit of cold meat. While she was running, Simon asked in a bad-tempered voice:

"Where the hell is Hilda?"

"On her holiday at Margate"

"Well, wire for her, can't you? That old woman gets on my nerves. You might have thought of wiring for Hilda."

"I don't know why I should be expected to think of wiring for Hilda. Why shouldn't you?"

"How in the name of God can I wire for Hilda when I don't know the damn girl's address?"

"Oh, for Christ's sake stop saying 'Wire for Hilda.'"

We sat in a tired silence until the policeman's widow popped back with some pressed beef and two bottles of beer. As we began to eat, I thought irrelevantly: "Torcello is still there. San Francesco and that funny little *Gasthaus* among the pines are still there." It seemed so incredibly funny that I had to press my napkin against my mouth. Simon looked up.

"What's the matter?"

"Nothing."

I pressed the napkin hard against my mouth, and suddenly the laughter changed to tears. I was sobbing uncontrollably, my head on the table-cloth. Simon was trying to comfort me, and the old terrier was standing by like a little white barrel on tooth-picks, wheezing and watching us with prominent black eyes.

❧

The funeral was next day at the Putney Vale Cemetery. I did not go. I went to the memorial service, and lunched at Prince's Gate afterwards. Men may come and men may go, but nothing can shake the sacred rites of food. And nothing short of an earthquake, it seemed, would ever disturb the expensive hideousness of this dining-room. There were the Chippendale chairs; the Dutch oysters and pomegranates. Tobacco-brown velvet framed the familiar view of Prince's Gate in hot midday sunshine.

But Mrs. Quinn had changed. She looked years older, and for a moment I felt almost sorry for her. She had been wonderful with Adrian, who had gone to pieces completely and was still too ill to see anyone. Yes, she would be wonderful in that sort of crisis. Her strength was like steel, her energy inexhaustible; whereas Adrian, so like her bodily, was straw under the steel. He had crumpled up, poor Adrian.

My father-in-law, still dapper about the shoulders, but more than usually silent, sat caressing his depressed moustache, as though he hoped to win it over by kindness into showing some life. I think that he was glad to have us there. For a moment it struck me that when I thought of the Quinns it was Mrs. Quinn who came into my mind; my hatred of them was not collective, but personal. Old Edward was merely a cipher in his own house, and I was sorry for him. Adrian did not count. Of the three of them, it was only that hard-faced, colourless woman at the head of the table who had personality. Disturbing thought! I came back in time to hear her say:

"Dr. Erskine called in a specialist at once, but—"

"Did you say Dr. Erskine?"

I remembered our argument about Lawrence at this table. It seemed years ago. The glossy red face, those dreadful little consulting-room jokes! "Now come along, my dear young lady; you're not going to die yet, you know. Don't be frightened; we'll soon put you right. ..." Had Gwen been frightened?

The pretty parlourmaid, looking subdued, was bending over me with a silver dish of apple-charlotte. I shook my head, speechless. Mrs. Quinn took me upstairs to see the new baby. It lay in a frilled cot, an ugly little human larva, opening and shutting its mouth as though in protest. That speck had murdered Gwen as effectively as a firing-squad. I looked at it in cold dislike. I made up my mind never to have a child. Life was unbearable. I wanted to be back in the Engadine, lying among the flowers, listening to the grasshoppers and the little green torrents.

※

The maids came back, annoyed at being torn away from the sylvan joys of Margate and Bognor. Hilda's nose was peeling.

"What about dinner, m'm?"

"I don't care. Anything you like."

"Mrs. Plum has left the scullery dreadful, and that dog of hers—you wouldn't believe—"

"I don't expect I should, Hilda."

"No, m'm. The butcher has left a bill for two weeks of James' bones we never had."

Oh, to hell with James' bones! What does it matter? But I tried to listen to Hilda patiently and rationally; I tried to think that she was a human being and not an ignorant animal who was perhaps slightly more valuable than a cow. The effort depressed me. I went upstairs, and the telephone rang.

"Oh, Miss Falconer? So glad you're back. Listen. The *Daily Magnet* would be interested in a thousand-word article from you on *Home Life Is Best*."

"No. ... I can't. I'm ill. I'm going away."

On my desk was a pile of books and papers that I had taken just as they were out of the suitcase. Sackville-West's *The Edwardians* (Simon had actually read it and liked it. I had teased him and said that he ought to have been Simon the Squire, with a place like Chevron); one of the best short novels in the world, *The Duel,* by Tchehov (that picnic where they all eat fish soup near the Tartar's *duhan*); *Little Mexican* and Flecker's poems. I had read *Little Mexican* lying on my bed in the hot Venetian siesta hour. It all seemed so long ago. Nothing was real now but the pavements, the sunburn on Hilda's nose, the washing hanging out next door, the two weeks' bones that we never had. The aerial domes and spires were unsubstantial as a dream.

I picked up *The Duel* listlessly, and there was the pad that I had bought at the corner of the Piazza. It was untouched. On the top page was written "Chapter I." And then had come the knock at the door, the 'cellos had faded away, and Gwen was lying dead of septic poisoning. I had not thought of the book since then. It would not really matter if I never thought of it again. But just for a moment I felt an awful stab of pain, a wrench of quite appalling misery. It was queer that Gwen, who alive had affected me not at all, should by dying put me on the edge of a nervous breakdown. Not only nervous breakdown— titanic breakdown of everything.

I thought: "I must get away quickly. If I don't get away I shall never be able to write again. It was all a mistake. These people don't belong to me; even Simon isn't my sort really. I'm allowing myself to become involved. I'm being drawn into their lives and hopelessly tangled up with them. They will crush me, slowly and surely. It's got to stop!"

But I continued to sit there, aimlessly drawing profiles on the pad. They all had a straight nose and a stubborn chin like Simon. Repeated a dozen times over, they seemed to close round those two solitary symbols of my dead book, to blot it out, to threaten it. "Chapter I." I looked at it for a long time.

Katie's footsteps sounded on the stairs. She was coming down from changing her dress. I heard her peculiarly penetrating sniff outside the door; she had perpetually inflamed nostrils and long teeth like a rabbit's.

"Lunch is served, m'm."

I looked round the little dining-room as though I were a stranger. Its yellow walls seemed fresh and attractive; I was pleased with the cunning arrangement of mirrors that tossed the reflections of Katie's brisk figure backwards and forwards across the room. She held a dish over my shoulder. What in the name of God possessed Hilda to give me stuffed onions to-day? After a few mouthfuls I laid down my fork, feeling suddenly hopeless and miserable. Katie was standing at the sideboard, with her back to me, opening drawers and taking out some silver. I looked at her neat waist, her strong legs in black silk stockings, and I was seized with a devouring curiosity to know what she felt about life. I thought of the queer, secretive existence that servants lead, huddled together in basements like a strange breed of burrowing animals, baffling and incomprehensible. There, two yards away from me, is another human being. I pay her forty-eight pounds a year; the social system under which we find ourselves allows me to lie in bed while she does the drawing-room fireplace; her mind is probably shallow, commonplace and vulgar, yet standing there she is as far from me and as mysteriously remote as some icy spur of the Himalayas.

"Katie."

"Yes, m'm?"

"Do you ever feel that you want to scream?"

She looked at me in surprise, then in acute embarrassment, turning her neck from side to side as though the neat lawn collar were too tight.

"Want to scream, m'm?"

"Yes, Katie, to scream." I was wrong; the experiment isn't going to be a success.

"Why, I don't know, m'm, I'm sure."

Her face, suspicious and resentful, seemed to relax. The attitude of her body became easier; for the first time I noticed that she had really beautifully-marked eyebrows that looked as though they had been flecked over with a brush dipped in oil.

"Sometimes I do get a bit fed up, and then I take it out of Hilda. Ever since I was a kid I've had a shocking temper, but Hilda and me get on all right."

"Hilda's the placid type."

"That's right, m'm. I often tell her it's soft to be so good-natured. People aren't going about giving you something for nothing in this world."

"I daresay you're right."

I should never be able to look at her again without seeing those beautiful eyebrows first. She lingered, looking at me rather anxiously, but I was occupied with the surprising fact that Katie, who worked hard for forty-eight pounds a year and admired Norma Shearer "ever so," should be tolerably contented; while I, to whom life had given every opportunity to recognise the true and love the beautiful, had reached a point where the whole thing seemed monstrously pointless. I had heard Beethoven and seen Venice, but I was not so happy as Katie, who thought Norma Shearer the pinnacle, the "ever so" of beauty. Katie got "a bit fed up" and "took it out of" the nearest human punching ball. I couldn't take it out of anyone, this hurt, angry, shut-up feeling in the chest. It was about Gwen, and yet not about Gwen. Perhaps it had started with Gwen and ended with myself. The destruction of something so lovely had shaken my belief in life. I felt that nothing could ever be the same again.

Katie was at my elbow with a bowl of stewed plums. Stuffed onions and stewed plums—I must say something about this to-morrow, very tactfully. Katie was still at my elbow.

"Hilda was saying to me that she's never seen you look so pale, m'm. Directly she seen you when we got back from our holidays she said to me, 'I've never seen madam look so pale.'"

Her nose, sharpened with solicitude, seemed more inflamed than ever. For a moment the spongy, sentimental side of me that responds to cheap music and old men with wooden legs was pleased. I clutched gratefully at the thought that they cared enough about me to discuss how I was looking as they sat downstairs in their comfortable wicker chairs, while Hilda's canary jangled and hopped in his brass cage overhead. Katie was saying that what I wanted was a nice change.

"But I've just had a change, Katie. We've been abroad, you know."

"Oh, abroad!" With one word she swept aside the pine forests and wrecked the airy dome of Maria del Salute. "Why don't you try Bognor one week-end, m'm? Or Bognor Regis, they call it now ever since the King was there that time. They've got ever such a nice front."

"Have they?"

I was suddenly bored and impatient. I didn't care a damn, really, what she thought about anything. All I wanted was—what? More than anything, at the moment, to be left in peace. I pushed back my chair.

"Don't worry, Katie. I'm perfectly all right, really. Bring coffee into the other room."

I lit a cigarette and lay down on the sofa. It had begun to

rain. All the colours of my little room were deadened by the gloomy yellowish light; the greens seemed like a sickly echo of the pre-Raphaelite era; the Venetian mirror reflected a strip of window and the clothes-line next door. There hung about everything that peculiar depression, that sense of having come suddenly to a dead end, that one gets at two o'clock on a wet afternoon in town. I looked at the little mirror and thought of sharp, bright colours; hot sunlight; gardens set cunningly like little oases of green in sunbaked walls. I thought of one evening when Simon and Marcus and I had been coming back from the Lido, and in that sudden condensation of colours that takes place just before dusk the water had turned a clear, dissolving peacock-green; out of it Venice seemed to spring like an iridescent bubble that some god had blown in one mighty breath. At a distance one could not distinguish terra-cotta from pink, pink from grey; the tall, thin palazzos shone a luminous white painted with ice-blue shadows. The air was so miraculously clear that our faces turned towards the city, seemed luminous too, mysteriously transfigured and bright. We sat in the launch, not speaking, three Botticelli angels holding wet bathing-suits. And I remembered that it was Simon, not Marcus, who seemed to share the loveliness of the moment; Simon who turned from contemplation of that aerial city and gave a sigh of profound, unutterable content. ...

The rain was making a dry, rustling noise. I thought that I would get up and put a record on the gramophone, a nice gay one; ring up someone; go out and walk very fast round the Serpentine. I continued to lie on the sofa. James, who had returned from the kennels that morning and was now dreaming of some recent hunting expedition, uttered a soft yelp. His paws lashed out, his black muzzle quivered. In imagination he was running through coarse, tussocky grass, with a white scut bobbing ahead; he was gaining on it, tongue dripping excitement; he was. ... He sat up, looked foolish and apologetic, and committed a social error.

A taxi was drawing up outside the door. I heard the squelch of its wheels and the *ping* of the meter-flag. The front-door bell rang. For some reason I thought, "My God, it's Mrs. Quinn!" I felt that I could not bear to have her rustling into the room like bamboos in a hot wind, talking of Gwen, looking disapprovingly at my waistline. Katie's sniff sounded from the hall. I jumped up to tell her that I was out, in Spain, dead; but it was too late.

The door opened, and Marcus came in.

I said stupidly:

"Oh, Marcus, I'm so glad to see you. I thought it was my mother-in-law!"

It seemed years since we had left him waving on the platform at Venice. He was carrying a bunch of pale yellow roses and two books in crisp new wrappers. The roses were for me, the books for himself. I looked at the titles. One was by Theodore Dreiser, and Marcus began talking of Dreiser, whom he knew very well. He said nothing of me, nothing of Venice or why we had left so suddenly. By some miracle the air of the room seemed to get warmer, the colours richer and more intense. I felt a sudden rush of relief and well-being. It was almost as though my nerves, that for days had been stretched out taut like strands of elastic, were snapping back one by one into place.

Presently he said:

"By the way, I'm not sailing on the *Bremen*, after all."

"Why not?"

"I've changed over to the *Leviathan*, which sails in a

fortnight. I can't wait longer than that. The New York office are beginning to send restive cables." He laughed. "I've got another fortnight in which to make you change your mind and come too."

"I've never been nearer to saying that I would."

"Well, why not?"

"I don't know. It's such an upheaval. I hate upheavals. I'm just in the state of mind when I want to be left alone to moulder quietly."

"What about the new book?"

"Done for. Bust. Gone up in smoke. There's not a shred of ambition left in me."

"That sounds pretty bad."

He got up and walked over to the window. For a minute he stood there, silently looking out; then he turned abruptly as though he had come to some decision, walked back to the sofa, and pulled me to my feet.

"Come along, let's go and look at some pictures. It isn't raining any more. I feel that I want to look at pictures. Then we'll go some place and have tea."

He looked down at my hand, straightened out the fingers, and put his mouth to the open palm. The contact startled me. His lips were warm and strong; I looked at his bent head and noticed the rather coarse graining of his skin, the thick black hair springing up exuberantly on either side of its parting. I looked with a slight, inexplicable feeling of dismay. Something passed like lightning through my mind and out again before I could lay hold of it. I said uncertainly:

"Your roses will die. I'd better put them in water."

Marcus doubled up my fingers again, gave them a sort of exasperated shake, and turned away.

"Yes," he said, and laughed. "Go along and put your roses in water."

I got home at half-past six. Simon was back from the office, sitting in the big arm-chair with a whisky-and-soda in his hand, and looking angrily at the Stock Exchange prices in the *Standard*. He said, without looking up:

"My God, if this goes on we'll be in the workhouse. Where the hell have you been?"

"Having tea with Marcus."

"Oh, so he's back?"

"Rather obviously."

"Snap, snarl, snap! Just like a cross little pug-dog, aren't you?"

"No, I'm not."

I thought: "Of all the damsilly conversations I've ever heard ours are easily the worst." I went upstairs and took off my hat. The Madonna had been taken out of the stocking-drawer and was in place over the bed again. I had a moment's envy of her blue-and-white placidity, and then I remembered the Frari Madonna who had reminded me of Gwen. I thought miserably: "Oh, God, what a mess!" Simon came into the room. He picked me up in his arms and sat down on the bed.

"Poor baby, so cross and so sweet. Do you know that I adore you?"

I said feebly:

"Everything's so beastly, Simon."

"I know."

And, strangely enough, I felt that he did know. He understood. It was strange that Simon, who could irritate me to the point of throwing books at his head, should be able to share the mysterious loveliness of that moment when we saw Venice hanging, an iridescent bubble between red day and blue twilight; it was strange that without speaking a word he could make me feel that he understood, perhaps a little better than I did, exactly what was going on in my bewildered brain. I wanted to tell him that I would never be able to write again if I didn't do something quickly: get away from the Quinns, or scream, or make some sort of stand. But it was too difficult to make the effort. Meanwhile it was nice to lie there quietly, not speaking, not even thinking.

Gradually the outside world flowed back. There was the chink of hot-water cans from the bathroom; I smelt roast mutton. Simon said:

"Feeling better? I tell you what, after dinner we might go and see Greta Garbo in some damn awful film. That will cheer you up like anything."

XI

࿉

I tried to pretend that I was working very hard. I soothed the wounded feelings of the *Daily Magnet* and told them that they should have their thousand words on the subject of "Home Life is Best." And in floods of passionate conviction I asserted that home-life was indubitably best; I deplored the modern tendency to live in restaurants and not by the domestic fireside; I pointed out the prosperity of the Victorian era, due, not to industrial advance and the development of the Empire, but— how did you guess?—to the fact that our grandfathers made their homes the kernel of their existence.

"For God's sake, Simon, this house is getting on my nerves. Let's go and dine at Quaglino's."

The *Daily Magnet* were pleased with the article. They brought it out with a large photograph of "Miss Nevis Falconer, the rising young novelist," taken when I was seventeen, looking bovine, with a pigtail down my back. I looked at the glaring type of my name and tried to feel pleased. I didn't feel pleased. But the *Daily Magnet* was enthusiastic, and asked me to say what I thought of "Modern Girls and Marriage, and What I Shall Teach My Child About Sacred and Profane Love." When I came to think of it, there was absolutely nothing to say about modern girls and marriage, or what I was going to teach my child about sacred and profane love. There could never have been anything to say. But I sat down at my desk and wrote two thousand passionately sincere words. It was like a rather pleasant substitute for drug-taking, with no harmful after-effects. I showed the articles to Marcus, and Marcus swore loudly.

At least it was better than spending numb hours staring at a blank page. I tried that for two mornings, I had some sort of hope that the book which had seemed so real, so living in the darkness of the little opera-house would creep out of the oblivion into which Gwen's death had sent it. While the violins formed one phrase, that book had been written; its final word penned. And then some strange accident of the brain had overtaken and destroyed it. Try as I would, I could not bring back the breath of life; the flesh and bones were still there, but the sensitive spirit had fled.

The people next door were still away, and workmen were in possession of the house. Every now and then one of them would come into the back garden and, looking up, call "Oi, Bill!" Bill would look over the edge of the roof and reply, "Oi!" Then Bill's friend, satisfied that no harm had come to him, would go back into the house and begin hitting something violently with a bit of old iron. This went on until twelve o'clock. I thought of going in and making a row, but whenever I looked out of the window they were sitting round drinking tea out of tin mugs, looking so pathetic and ridiculous, so like a lot of amiable old walruses in paint-smeared aprons, that I always went hopelessly back to my desk again.

On the second morning the door was thrown open, and Hilda came into the room like a shell from a gun. Behind her was Katie, red in the face and breathing hard. Hilda said:

"Please, m'm, I think I'd better give in my month's notice. I can't stay in the house a minute longer with Katie, m'm; her temper is that shocking bad I'm afraid she'll do me an injury."

Katie said indignantly:

"Well, I never! What a thing to say!"

"My young man says I ought to have given in my notice long ago. I'm getting that jumpy I can't give proper attention to my cooking. It's not that I'm not happy here, m'm, even though the stairs take it out of you dreadful and all those fancy egg-dishes you like for lunch and all. I'm not a one for grumbling but I've stood as much as I can from Katie and her cheek, m'm, and that's a fact."

Katie burst into tears. I looked at Hilda's tightly-compressed lips and flashing glasses, and was conscious only of a faint feeling of surprise that her young man should have emerged from his chronic speechlessness long enough to tell her that she ought to give in her notice. Did she take off her glasses when he kissed her? I had seen Hilda once without her glasses, and her eyes had looked lost, frightened, like pale little fishes that begged gaspingly to be put back in their aquarium again. ... I came back with a start to find them looking at me expectantly, and a vast exasperation possessed me. What did I care if Hilda went or stayed, lived or fell dead before me? I said:

"Well, I'm sorry you feel like that, Hilda. If you really feel that you can't get on with Katie, you'd better go, of course. But I think you ought to think it over first."

They both looked taken aback. Katie said tearfully that she knew she had a wicked temper, but it was better over and done with quickly than hanging on for days like some people's. Her inflamed nostrils quivered. I resisted a sudden temptation to get up and knock their heads together. I said:

"All right, Hilda. If you think better of it, come and tell me. If not, I'll take it that you're leaving a month from to-day."

I turned back to the desk, and they went away, for the

moment united by their common contempt of me. I made an effort to collect my thoughts, but the air was jagged and quivering with Hilda's anger and Katie's sobs; I found myself still ridiculously preoccupied with the problem of the glasses. From next door came a hoarse shout:

"Oi, Bill!"

"Oi!"

A street musician with a cigar-box fiddle sat down opposite the house and began to play "I Kiss Your Hand, Madame."

※

London in September. The leaves were falling in the parks; the dahlias warmed the heart with their soft yellows, their biting magentas and scarlets. There were days of rain, mingled with bursts of thin, ironic sunlight that seemed to give the streets something of the gaiety of Paris. I never loved London more than in those last two weeks. London, my London! The big squares with their space and dignity; the keen autumn smell; the people in the streets, hurrying along as though their northern blood responded to this new stir in the air; dogs running in the grass and soft, dahlia-coloured stuffs glowing behind plate-glass; the slow good-humour, the patience, the steady beat of the city's life. One day I took James in the Green Park for a run, and there behind me, sharp in the evening sunlight against a powdery blue sky, rose the old grey houses and the new white palaces of Piccadilly; the distances of grass, trees and houses were miraculously clear. Some children raced by, red-cheeked, bowling hoops, and over my head, with a crisp whir, fled three wild ducks making for the St. James's Park lake.

I felt suddenly happy and at peace. I sat down on a green

chair and thought, "Why can't life always be like this?" The evening was so pure and calm. In a moment, if I continued to sit here quietly, I might find out the answer to everything. It was one of those evenings. I looked down from following the flight of the wild ducks, and saw a hideously old, hideously battered and inhuman shape lying a few hundred yards away from me under the trees. It lay perfectly still, its arms and legs thrown in queer, limp positions, as though they were stuffed with sawdust, its soiled white face turned up to the sky. Some of its fellows were dotted about the grass; one or two were sitting up and making slow, sodden gestures; others were standing propped up against trees, heads hanging like patient horses.

The evening was pure and calm no longer. I felt angry and miserable. I looked in my bag; there was a pound note and some silver. The shape on the grass turned its dead, incurious eyes towards me. I thrust the money into its dirty hand and said angrily: "Here, for God's sake take this and go and get something to eat." It made some sort of sound. Its face looked expressionless, featureless, as though it had been underground for a long time and someone had just dug it up; a patient, earthy look. I glanced round as I walked quickly away, and there were the other shapes crawling over the grass towards it, slowly and inexorably, like cockroaches who have just seen a crust of bread.

I said: "Oh, God!"

But presently I was vaguely comforted by the thought that I should never become a proper Quinn so long as I went about giving pound notes to beggars in the Park. The Quinns never gave money to beggars, because it was well-known that most beggars were richer than they were and only went about looking hungry for fun. But they subscribed heavily to all the best charities, and if they subscribed often enough they were given titles, which was nice for their children. I felt vaguely comforted, even when I discovered that I had not left myself enough money to get a new jar of face-cream.

That brought us to Saturday. Marcus was sailing in a week; he had gone over to Paris again for the week-end and would be back on Monday. On Saturday morning the telephone-bell rang and Cora's faint, husky voice implored us to pack a suitcase with our oldest clothes and go down to Burnham Beeches for the week-end.

"There's nobody else staying in the house and it will probably pour with rain. If you feel that you can stand such excitement, do come."

"We'll be down for lunch, Cora."

It poured with rain. The Michaelmas daisies in Frank's garden stood in sodden stacks, their watery mauve plumes bowed down to the earth with moisture; the plummy red of the brick wall against which fruit-trees were nailed with fluttering bits of rag, the dead gold of the dripping woods were blurred and softened by a veil of rain. The earth was sweet and rotten with decay. In the evening a white vapour rose from the ground; in it the familiar shapes of trees disappeared, the lawn became a steaming lake; slow wisps of mist curled menacingly round the house. And as though by magic, fires appeared and lamps glowed in the rooms. We sat secure in a little citadel of summer while autumn prowled outside, shaking the window-panes with gusts of irritable fury.

It was always restful at Red Court. There were times when I wondered whether Cora hadn't done a wise thing in turning her back on the Big Satisfying Gestures. When I compared the peace of her house with the eternal chaos of Montpelier Place it seemed to me that it was better to be a success at one thing than to try, as I was trying, to be a success at several things. I wondered if Simon was doing some comparing too. I noticed him looking round contentedly now and then, as though he liked the white walls and soft-coloured Persian rugs, the great walnut press, the flowers with which Cora always surrounded herself. And the meals were punctual, and the butler never came in to say that they had run right out of coffee. Oh, dear!

After lunch Frank and Simon went off in the car to play golf, saying hopefully that it was going to clear up. The children insisted that Cora and I should be shown a new walk through the woods. They tore ahead and ran back to us, full of ceaseless indomitable energy; three small human engines in mackintoshes and bright scarlet berets. Their shrill voices rose triumphantly over the dripping of the wet boughs and the surf of dead leaves that murmured under our feet. Often they ran back, full of excitement and noisy affection, to push into our hands a spray of extremely damp leaves or a draggled blue feather. It amused me to see how Cora treated them—with a detached, ironic sense of humour, as though they were beings of an equal intelligence to herself. One felt that she would be marvellously comforting in crisis of chicken-pox and sprained ankles, but that her maternal solicitude would never be overpowering; she would always be more interested in them as human beings than as children and her own particular property. They adored her.

And I thought as we followed them at a more sedate pace that I should never love another woman as I loved Cora. We were not particularly demonstrative. We rarely kissed; we never, metaphorically speaking, took off our corsets, let down our hair, and had a cosy little exchange of girlish confidences. We were both tremendous respecters of privacy. I don't think I had ever told her in so many words that I was fonder of her than of any one in the world except Simon. We never seemed to notice the fourteen years' difference between us. She understood everything without being told; she was so gay, so keen and interested and tolerant. Dear Cora.

I thought how peaceful it was, how deeply satisfying, to forget about men for a moment and walk with another woman in a wood, the children running round us. This was a relationship in which there was nothing hurtful, nothing unkind, and something profoundly good. And I reflected on those lovely little Italian pictures of two women sitting with a child between them. Sometimes the women are Madonna and Saint, the Child between them is an infant Christ or a curly-headed St. John; sometimes there are stiff flowers in the picture, or the air is rich with cherubim; sometimes they are just two simple women sitting at the close of a long, hot day, watching a sleeping child. But always there is peace in their faces and the curve of their bodies. They seem bound together in a communion that is sexless and ageless; to be strong with secrets of content that men can never know.

I thought: "If I could go away alone with Cora for a bit, everything would come right." I thought of a cottage in Cornwall or Dorsetshire; long walks like this, and reading, and endless talks. But Cora could not leave Frank and go careering off to cottages in Cornwall. And out of the long silence I told her suddenly that I might be going to New York. The words rather startled me; up to that moment I had not thought seriously of the idea at all. Cora did not look surprised. She asked:

"When do you go?"

"Oh, it's not so definite as that. Nothing's definite."

"I see."

"It would be such an absolute change, a beginning all over again. I feel that I want something like that. I feel that wherever I turn there's a blank wall. Ever had that feeling, Cora? No, of course you haven't. You're like Gwen was—contented."

Cora was silent, picking her way thoughtfully among the wet leaves. I said rather desperately:

"It would be all right if Simon and I had lots of paternal and maternal instincts. We'd have had a baby by now, and there'd be something to concentrate on, something to use up my surplus energy."

"Want one?"

"I don't know. Sometimes I do and sometimes I don't. And that's rather the way of everything. We've been married four years; sometimes we're happy, sometimes we're not. I don't like housekeeping, and I can't even write any more. Everything's static. I've been moving in the same damnable little circle for the last four years, Cora. It's time something blew me up or out, or to the devil—I don't care which."

"I'm rather frightened about you, Nevis."

"Why? Oh, you needn't worry. This fine, reckless tone never lasts." But I came abruptly to a standstill and cried: "When I think how simple everything used to be! I knew what I wanted, I knew that I was going to write the most marvellous book in the world! What's happened to everything? What's changed?"

"You've changed, Nevis. Growing up a bit, that's all. Uncomfortable, but necessary."

We turned towards home again, heavily laden with leaves and blue feathers and pinky-orange spindleberries. The children were tired now; they lagged behind and were a little quarrelsome.

"What do you think about it, Cora?"

"If you feel that you must go, there's nothing more to be said, my dear. You're the important one, always. I don't want you to be influenced by any one—Simon or me or your friend Marcus Chard."

I insisted:

"But what do you feel about it? You must feel something."

She was silent. Her small, colourless face was marked deeply with lines of thought; for a moment, the animation gone from it, it looked plain and tired. I thought with a faint shock: "Cora is thirty-eight." We had left the woods now and were walking down a muddy lane with a brake of dark Scotch firs rising steeply on either side. She said slowly:

"I feel that whatever comes of it will have some sort of meaning. Nothing is meaningless. That, so far as I've got a religion, is my religion, Nevis. You may go away and have an experience that will hurt you, but after a while you will find that it has had its value in your life, even though it may have been a queer, unhappy one."

It began to rain with renewed vigour; big drops rattled like musketry among the trees. The children, gathering fresh supplies of energy, squealed their delighted horror. We seized their hands and ran for our lives down the lane to the shelter of the Red Court orchard wall. When we arrived, hot and breathless, bits of moss and leaves in our untidy hair, we saw that a blue car was standing outside the front door. People had come to tea.

They stayed for an hour and a half. They were nice people, gentle and kindly; distinguished in a dowdy way, traditional and unexciting. Indian Army, you know, and punkah-wallahs and dinners at Viceregal Lodge, but disguised now in the civilian ease of tweeds and nicely-worn brown shoes. "And how is your celery doing, Mrs. Fenton?" I looked at Cora, and saw that she was treating them beautifully. She had come straight into the drawing-room as she was; she sat there, still in her muddy shoes, her slim knees crossed and a cigarette between her lips, talking a lot of outrageous nonsense and looking elegant as a porcelain figure. The General listened, his very bright blue eyes twinkling. The tea-table shone with glass jars of honey and jam, with china sprigged in a clean pattern of green and white.

I thought: "How easy life is for these people." There was a daughter, too. Thirty-one or two; good eyes and teeth; large hands that, later, she plunged decisively into doeskin driving-gloves. She did things to dogs, and ought to have been married. Simon, back from golf, stood over her and listened gravely while she talked about curing canker in cocker spaniels. His fairness looked red in the firelight. I knew that attentive expression so well, that grave and deferential interest in the middle of which he would look swiftly across the room at me and smile. He had the animal's instant consciousness of being watched. But to-day, perversely or by chance, he did not look up and give me that secret little smile. I felt irritated and rebuffed. I heard him say:

"Well, that's damn interesting. I've always had the best results with the powder, myself. You take—"

"When are you going to give us another book, Mrs. Quinn?"

I thought drearily, "Oh, hell!" If one happens to be a professional writer, there are always people who make a point of enquiring about one's new book as though it were a child just recovering from scarlet fever. "How is the new book going?" Anxiety, polite interests, two pounds of the best black grapes.

"Very nicely, thank you. We expect it to live now." "Oh, I'm so glad! That's splendid!" And, the unpleasant duty over, away the enquirer trips, *so* relieved, *so* thankful that the dear little sufferer is out of danger and soon going to appear in a nice new seven-and-sixpenny jacket.

And then there are the damn fools who ask "How many words do you write in a day?" and "Do you have some sort of plan or carry it all in your head?" and "Now what does Gilbert Frankau get for a book? ..." I came back with a start. The question had been put so kindly; it was impossible to feel irritated with this gentle, vaguely benevolent lady whose faded eyes smiled at me from under a perched monstrosity of felt and jay's wings. I said:

"I don't think I shall ever write anything any more."

And ignoring her startled, cooing sounds of protest. ... "But such a *nice* book, *Vulcan's Harvest*—we all enjoyed it so much, didn't we, Dorothy?"—I felt the familiar misery rush over my body like physical pain. Dreams fade; gentle and beautiful things like Gwen are allowed to die in agony; one starts off reaching for the moon, and ends up facing a blank wall. I'm twenty-four, and there doesn't seem to be anything left but settling down and playing contract bridge and saying good-bye to Nevis Falconer. She was always a bit of a fool, anyway. Enter Nevis Quinn! ... I said blindly to the faded eyes below the jay's wings:

"I'm so glad you like it. Oh, I don't know. There doesn't seem to be anything left to write about. Yes, I may later on. Have you read *Bengal Lancer*?"

Presently they went away. The house was quiet again; the white walls, the gleam of old bronze and Persian rugs renewed their true values, unbroken by foreign intrusions. I went upstairs to our room. My white chiffon dress, stockings and crêpe under-things were laid out neatly on the bed. Life seems to be one long succession of meals and getting dressed for the next meal. The windows were wide open; it had stopped raining and the evening was quiet and sad; the earth seemed to be mourning, dumb, withdrawn into its grief like an animal.

What had Cora said? "You may go away and have an experience that will hurt you, but after a while you will find that it has had its value in your life, even though it may have been a queer, unhappy one." I felt that she had said something, but not everything, that she felt; she had dressed up the truth in words and evasions. The truth! There was only one person in the world who was ruthless enough to give me that. And swiftly I sat down at the writing-table, took a sheet of the thick grey paper and wrote "Dear Marcus." After that the words came easily, in an unbroken rush:

DEAR MARCUS,

I'm writing to you because writing always seems easier to me than talking. Perhaps I'm taking a little too much for granted. I'm taking for granted that you're fond of me and that, therefore, you care a little bit what happens to me. Oh, Marcus, I'm in such a muddle! Life seemed such gloriously plain sailing a little while ago, and now, I don't know why, it's all gone to hell.

What am I going to do? Shall I come to New York? Will it do any good, or am I a fool to think that crossing the Atlantic will work some kind of miracle, and instantly I shall know what I want, the spell will be broken, and back will come the urge to write again? Who cares if I do or don't write, anyway? Nobody knows better than I do that the world is too damnably full of promising young female novelists; books are entering the world at the rate of a thousand a minute, and ninety per cent of them ought to have been strangled at birth. If I never write another word it ought to be a case for hearty self-congratulation and drinks all round.

But that's all rot. I've got to write. Something inside me says that I've got to write, and go on writing as well as I know how, or else be utterly destroyed. It's as much a part of me as that. All this summer I've been happier because you were here, and knowing you seemed to give me back my self-confidence. Then something happened and it shrivelled up again. What happened? I must try to remember so that you'll be able to understand, Marcus.

Gwen died. Do you remember, when we were in Venice? It gave me a terrible shock. Somehow, in some queer way, it seemed like a symbol, a bad omen. It's difficult to explain, but try, please try to understand. You see, you don't know Simon really well, or his family. They're all so dominating, so strong in time they get you down and crush the life out of you. You have their children, and die, or else you live, but only a shadowy version of yourself with the Quinn individuality super-imposed on top. And I won't become shadowy, Marcus! I won't, won't, positively won't be crushed! Gwen gave up the struggle and died, and now I feel that all the Quinn energy will be concentrated on me. They won't be happy till they've turned me into a nice young Quinn matron with—what was that dismal prophecy you made in Venice? Yes, a baby-carriage and a Morris-Oxford car. And after that, I might as well be dead.

Tell me what to do. I believe in you. If you say come to New York, I'll come. If I go away for a bit and see a lot of new things I may find the strength of mind to come back and say to the

Quinns, "Be damned to you!" But I don't know. I'm miserable as hell. Write to me when you get back from Paris. Don't 'phone or come round to Montpelier Place. Write to me.

NEVIS.

I put the letter into an envelope and addressed it. I heard Simon come into the dressing-room next door; after a pause he went along the corridor to the bathroom. He strolled back, whistling; put his damp reddish head round the door and asked: "What are you going to wear tonight?"

"White chiffon."

"That's all right."

He went back, opened and shut drawers, went on whistling. What's that stupid tune? Crass, stupid, damned fool, you may be losing me for all you know, and you go on whistling. Oh, Simon, my darling, come in and tell me that you love me; tell me anything; hold me close and save me. What am I talking about? It's a funny thing, but Simon only tells me that he loves me at moments when I'm feeling cross or tired or ill; when I want to hear it, he goes on whistling.

I undressed and had a bath; I put on the crêpe underclothes, the long stockings, the white chiffon dress; I powdered and rouged and polished my nails and dabbed some scent at the parting of my hair. The letter to Marcus was lying on the mantelpiece. I thought: "Simon will see it when he comes in. If he asks me what's in it I will tell him, and if he doesn't want me to send it I will tear it up."

Simon came into the room, tying his tie. I sat and watched him in the mirror. He saw the letter on the mantelpiece; his eyes grew watchful, his expression seemed to tighten up. He said:

"Why the hell does Katie always put my clean shirts in the wash and keep my dirty ones for when I go away."

"I don't know."

"Damn the girl, anyway."

He strolled out again, whistling. I took the letter and went downstairs. The old butler was coming out of the dining-room. I said:

"Will you put this in the post for me, Albert?"

XII

We went back to town early on Monday morning. Katie, looking subdued, came down the steps and took the suitcases. There was a telephone message from Mrs. Quinn on the pad; no letters. I found myself wandering restlessly round the house after Simon had left. The little rooms were chillingly neat; there were no flowers, no papers or magazines littering the broad stool by the fireplace. The place seemed to have a strained, expectant look, as though it were waiting for something to happen. I thought suddenly: "I've never liked this house." Although Simon and I had loved each other so often here, although the walls had echoed with our fierce quarrels and fiercer reconciliations, I would be able to walk out at any time without a qualm. For some strange reason I had planted no roots here. It pleased me if people said that the house was attractive and admired the yellow dining-room, but that was all. I thought: "I'll get Simon to sell it. We'll go and live in the country and never come up to town. We'll take one of those new flats—I've always wanted a flat. We'll go abroad and buy a ranch in South America, and Simon can be happy breeding horses. Or, simpler still, we won't move at all. What does it matter?"

I had brought home some flowers from Red Court: great spiked dahlias and some late roses and feathery Michaelmas daisies, a deep lilac-pink with surprised yellow centres. I took a long time over the business of arranging them; holding them to my face; drawing a faint satisfaction and comfort from their bright shapes and the damp, earthy sweetness that breathed from their leaves. The house began to look a little warmer. I set the Michaelmas daisies where they would splash their colour in a shadowed corner. The rest of the morning stretched ahead, empty and endless.

There was Hilda waiting in the kitchen, with the orders slate in her hand.

"Please, m'm, Katie and me have been thinking it over, and if it's all the same to you, we'd like to stay on."

"Well, I'm glad you've made it up, Hilda."

"Yes, m'm. It's quite made up now. Katie's a good girl when her catarrh doesn't make her nervy. I'm sure we'd both be ever so sorry to leave you and Mr. Quinn."

Don't you believe it; you wouldn't be sorry at all. Yes, you might he sorry to leave Simon, because he treats you in the right way, but you don't like me. You despise me. Oh, what the hell does it matter? What does anything matter?

"The butcher's bill seems to be rather heavy, this week, Hilda."

I went upstairs and looked at the telephone-pad. Will Mr. and Mrs. Simon dine with Mrs. Quinn next Thursday, *quiet,* only the family? Oh, God! I sat down, lit a cigarette, and wondered if Marcus had got my letter.

His answer came in the late afternoon. The house seemed unbearable after lunch, and in desperation I went off to a cinema. The darkness was soothing. I drugged my mind with the stupidity and the incredible slackness of the thing, as one might take a couple of aspirins. The money that had been spent on its production would have bought a Rembrandt. Everything was so gorgeous; gorgeous American homes; gorgeous teeth;

gorgeous eyelashes like charred rope. In the middle of it all an actress recruited from the stage wandered about looking a little dazed. I thought of Marcus' story of the film-producer who said to him: "I want this production to be the most stupendous thing we've ever done. It's only colossal now."

I laughed, and the lady beside me rustled indignantly. On the screen someone was dying, gorgeously, of course, with the wraith of his gorgeous salary hovering complacently in the background. I wished that he would go on dying for ever, that the stupidity and the slickness would prolong themselves indefinitely, for while they did so I could not think. I could only feel. I was carried along in the darkness on a warm, easy tide of emotion. Oh, die for ever! Has Marcus got my letter yet?

I let myself into the house. Katie came sniffing up the stairs.

"Are you ready for tea, m'm? A District Messenger boy has just brought this."

It was like Marcus to think of sending an express letter. I ripped it open clumsily; the paper tore.

DEAR NEVIS,

I have taken the liberty of booking a passage for you provisionally on the *Leviathan*, which, as you know, sails on Saturday. Some friends are motoring me down to Southampton, so until we meet on the boat—

As ever,

M. C.

Remember what I said in Venice? The apartment is waiting for you. Don't disappoint me now.

"Yes, Katie, I'm quite ready for tea."

For a variety of reasons I remember that evening very well. The week-end of rain had put softness into the air; the pale, shining afternoon had died early in a sombre sunset, crimson streaked with dark bars of cloud that burnt for a while and then seemed to go out in a puff. Darkness arched over the houses, dense and softly shining, although there was no moon. I stood by the open window, feeling the silky air touch my cheek and forehead, and thought that I would always remember this evening because it was so beautiful. In one of the houses in Montpelier Square someone was playing the piano; Mozart, a bit of Debussy. I thought that I knew who it was. That slender, dark young woman with the painted mouth and the faintly bitter expression; I had seen her coming out of the house so often, nearly always dressed in black. She had a small white Chinese dog. She would be playing Mozart in the darkness, not looking at her slowly weaving hands but staring in front of her, bitter and unrelaxed; somewhere in the shadows a small white ghost would be curled up motionless, a porcelain wraith of a dog on a cushion of scarlet silk. ... People, people, people!

I leant farther out, as though to escape from the lighted room, from Simon's fair head shining under the lamp. Everything was so quiet, so soft and windless. I thought of a spring evening in the country, years ago, when I had been seized with a sudden fear that I would die because the world was so unbearably beautiful. The quiet sky, the cloud of plum-blossom against a wild moon, the thrilling spring air that seemed alive with faint, moist scents and rustling sounds—it was all too intense and aching to be borne. Something would come along and kill me off in the middle of the agony and rapture. I lay face downwards in the orchard, crushing the scatter of primroses, and prayed wildly: "Oh, God, please let me live! Please, please don't let me be run over or catch anything for Jesus Christ's sake Amen." And I was comforted, as I sat up and smelt the dark brown wall-flowers and saw the orchard trees stirring palely in the wash of moonlight, by a feeling that heaven had heard. Divine providence would see to it that the motor-'bus and the epidemic touched me not; an eternity of April orchards stretched luminous before me under the moon. ...

Years ago. I must have been fourteen or fifteen then, and now I was twenty-four. Things weren't agony and rapture any more, and I didn't say prayers. Prayers were only part of an outworn superstition. I was perfectly sure of that in the day-time; sometimes I forgot when I was frightened or there was a thunderstorm in the night. To experience agony and rapture again! What had Cora said? "Growing up a bit, that's all. Uncomfortable, but necessary. ..."

Simon stood behind me.

"What are you looking at?"

"Nothing."

I thought: "You'd better tell him now." All through dinner I had talked without stopping; I had heard my own voice rising and falling, saying things about the week-end and James and the servants and a book that I wanted to get. Simon had said practically nothing. He had leant back in his chair, fingering a wine-glass and watching me through his lashes.

"Simon,"—I turned round rather desperately. "It's such a lovely evening. Let's drive round the Park for a bit."

"All right. I'll go round and get the car. You'll want a coat or something, won't you?"

In my black velvet coat I felt part of the darkness. I slid softly into the seat by Simon's side and softly folded my pale hands in my lap. He muttered something angrily under his breath; the car was protesting against being taken out again. I shut my eyes. Cool air flowed towards me; lights battered in a blurred red wave against my closed lids. I felt the warmth of Simon's shoulder, and that made me think of the first time that I had ever driven in this car, four years ago; the warm grass smell and the hedges of wild roses, the little pub with its three tubs filled with marguerites. *Do you remember an Inn, Miranda?* But we had made the mistake of going back. One should never go back. *Never any more, Miranda, never any more.* I wanted to say: "Whatever happens I shall always remember that, Simon. Whatever happens I shall always love you. Deep down, under all the stupidity, we belong to each other."

I said:

"This is lovely, Simon."

We slid through the gates of the Park. Great shapes of trees stood silently in darkness, holding out their arms, and beneath them lean shadows with hungry white eyes sped to and fro, screaming a warning. Red lights peered out of the jungle at Hyde Park Corner. There was a faint, sad smell of dead leaves and earth. When we get to the dahlias at Lancaster Gate I'll tell him. The headlights gleamed on a white face; two white faces pressed against each other, tranced and still. They sat so quietly, the poor devils, bodies locked in each other's arms, breathing in the soft air and the musty autumn scents. By day they were probably mean, foolish and vulgar; by night they were mysteries in mystery. Terrible, the state of our parks. When we get to Albert Gate I'll tell him. I made a sudden nervous movement and cried:

"I wish we could get out and walk, Simon. I wish we were miles away from here, walking very fast under trees."

He asked:

"What do you want to tell me, Nevis?"

"How do you know that I want to tell you anything?"

He laughed.

"My God, I ought to know your face by now! What is it?"

"Simon. ..."

"Well, what is it?"

Knightsbridge Barracks loomed out of the darkness like a lighted ship. All those men in there: forlorn, coarse and pathetic in their echoing masculine rooms. What do soldiers do in the evenings? By day one sees them in the Park; nice red-faced boys, very tall in their high-waisted grey overcoats, leaning against the railings and talking to servant-girls.

> *On Monday*
> *I go out with a sol-jer;*
> *On Chewsday*
> *I go out with a ...*

"Simon, I'm going away for a bit. To New York."

He said:

"I see."

"Are you surprised?"

"No, I can't say that I'm surprised."

"We've always been believers in freedom, haven't we, Simon? I remember we agreed once that if one of us wanted to go off for a bit, the other wouldn't make a fuss or ask questions."

"I'm not going to ask questions."

No, damn you, I wish that you were. I wish that you'd

swear, crash the car, throw something at me—do anything and everything but sit there and continue to be absorbed in the twin beams of light ahead. I turned my head and looked at him. A street lamp gleamed on his profile and showed it white, thoughtful. Oh, Simon, my dearest, are you hurt? Angry?

"I decided all of a sudden. You know that's the way I always do things. Madly, in a rush. I ... booked a passage on the *Leviathan*."

"When does she sail?"

"Saturday."

"That's lucky. I'll be able to come down and see you off."

I started to laugh.

"Why are you laughing?"

"I don't know."

But I was laughing because it was so typical of Simon to exhibit no surprise at the news that I was going to America in five days' time. We were very alike in that way, accustomed to make sudden wild decisions, to arrange the next two years in as many minutes. A policeman stepped out of the shadows and held up his hand. The traffic surged to a standstill, panted a moment, surged forward again.

"I don't suppose that I'll be able to go to your mother's dinner on Thursday. There'll be so many things to do. It's going to be rather a rush—"

"Yes. She'll be surprised."

"I suppose she will, Simon."

I'm glad it's going to be a rush. Glad, glad! I don't want to think until Saturday; I want the week to gather itself together like a vast dark wave and carry me along, breathless and drowning, until it splinters against the rock of Saturday. Things to do, thank God. I clutched at them gratefully. I shall want a new tweed coat for the boat, my old one is rather …

"Simon, darling, it's the only possible solution at the minute. I've got into a muddle here. I can't work. I'm unhappy, so I want to be a coward and run away and leave it all. If I go away for a bit everything will straighten out."

"Are you coming back?"

I looked at him. He was still staring ahead, white and thoughtful. It was strange to see Simon thoughtful; his face was usually so vehemently occupied in expressing something—laughter or anger or passionate interest. When Simon laughed he threw back his head, his straight nose bent a little at the tip and his lashes flickered together. But Simon was not laughing now. I said:

"Yes, I'm coming back."

"When?"

"It's hard to say. Perhaps in a couple of weeks, perhaps in three months. I may not like it at all."

He said again: "I see," and was silent. I stared at the darkness of trees and grass, and tried to send my mind forward to meet the sudden reality, the staggering imminence of New York. Impossible! It remained a grin of sharp white teeth biting a jagged rent in the sky-line. And suddenly I felt young and afraid; I put out a hand and touched Simon's knee.

He looked at me and smiled.

"Poor little Nevis."

"Oh, Simon, you don't understand how much this ridiculous business of writing things down on bits of paper means to me. It's so much a part of me that if it goes wrong I go wrong too. You can't understand that."

He said:

"No, I can't understand that."

There was a sort of patient, dumb perplexity in his voice. I wanted suddenly to cry. I pressed his knee hard and said nothing. The night air lifted the hair off my forehead; it smelt damp and cool, as though it had come out of a cave in the rocks. We circled the Park once more. There had been an accident at Stanhope Gate; a red sports car had crashed into one of the islands. A lot of glass lay about in the road, and a policeman was busy writing in a note-book. Simon slowed down. He loved a good accident. He said:

"By God, that chap's done for himself! It must have only just happened."

I glanced vaguely at the broken glass.

"Are you going to get out and look?"

"No, I don't think so." He sounded rather regretful. "It's not really worth it. God, did you see that wind-screen?"

"Yes."

He seemed to have recovered his spirits at a leap. I felt chilled and irritated. I thought: "You won't even miss me." He went on talking cheerfully about the accident. Suddenly he said:

"I suppose you'll be seeing a good deal of Chard in New York?"

"I suppose so, yes."

"Isn't he sailing on the *Leviathan*, too?"

"Yes."

"You like him, don't you? He can talk books and all the rest of it. He understands you."

"Yes. He's a kind person, Simon."

"I believe he is, in his way. Of course you like him. So do I, for that matter."

He brought his hand down heavily on the wheel, and the

horn screamed. We turned out of the gates at Hyde Park Corner. A 'bus loomed over us, packed tightly with swaying bodies; the pale faces swayed, too, all languid and musing, turned inwards on their own secret hopes and desires. For a moment they stared down at us, incurious white discs pasted against glass. The car slid into a quiet street and gathered speed.

I glanced sideways at Simon's profile. It was alert and absorbed, lips obstinately compressed, the eyes shadowed by an old felt hat that was slanted at an angle peculiarly Simon's. And suddenly I was weak with love and tenderness. His excitement over the accident, which had irritated me so much ten minutes ago, now seemed merely pathetic. He was like all men: childish, egotistical, ruthless, sensual and forlorn. He was like no other man, for he was mine. He was my child, and I could not leave him. Could I leave him? And my eyes filled with tears, for I had found out that I was just a little harder than I had thought. I could and would leave him. The *Leviathan* was sailing on Saturday.

I said quickly:

"Simon, I'm going to New York to see if I can write a book. It's something that's *got* to be written, but the moment it's finished I'll rush home. You'll get a cable: 'Meet me at Southampton in five days, hurrah!'"

"All right."

"I'll be thinking of that cable all the time, Simon."

He was silent.

I looked up at the sky and wondered how I could have thought that this evening was tranquil and beautiful. It was sad, achingly sad. Its sadness pressed down like a heavy dark weight on the houses, and all the people sat inside, surrounded by the defensive gaiety of lamps and music and soft colours, pretending not to know. A warm drop of rain fell softly on my hand as we turned into Montpelier Place. No Mozart came floating out of the darkness now; the house was shuttered and silent. I still sat in the car, looking up at Simon. But his face was shuttered and silent too; he had retreated into himself; he was utterly withdrawn.

"Simon."

"Yes?"

After all, there is nothing to say.

"All right. Nothing. Don't be too long at the garage."

While we undressed we discussed passports, money arrangements, and whether Hilda could be trusted to manage the housekeeping if I was not there to get in her way for ten minutes every morning.

❧

The next day there were things to do. People to telephone, clothes to buy, the *Leviathan* booking to be confirmed at Cook's.

"You have to get a United States visa, you know."

"Yes." I looked at the clerk's sunburnt face—he must have just come back from his annual holiday. He was so matter-of-fact about it all, so deadly matter-of-fact. He tapped his gold fillings reflectively with a pencil and then, transferring the pencil to a chart, caroled:

"Here we are! Very nice cabin, madam, *and* a bathroom."

He stabbed the pencil triumphantly into a nice little drawing of a toilet-seat.

"Oh, yes," I looked at it vaguely. "It seems all right."

"Oh, I'm sure you'll be comfortable there," he said bracingly, adjusting his horn-rimmed glasses with the tip of a nicotine-stained finger.

I went out into the sunshine again. What next? There was that tweed coat to be bought, and I wanted a pair of sports shoes for walking on deck. And after that. ...

XIII

It was raining in Southampton and they told us that the *Levia-than* was delayed by fog. The tenders would not be leaving before eight o'clock. Eight o'clock! I looked at Simon blankly. I had been all keyed up to take the plunge, to walk up the gangplank and think: "Well, thank God that's over!" It was like keying oneself up to jump off the Eiffel Tower and then, with one foot in mid-air, being told "You can't jump off before eight o'clock."

"What in the world are we going to do?"

"We might sit here for a bit and have some coffee."

We sat and watched my fellow-passengers wandering aimlessly round the lounge. They, too, had slightly disconcerted airs as though they were annoyed at finding themselves still high and dry on the Eiffel Tower. One or two sat at side tables and feverishly wrote out Western Union cablegrams. Two little American boys, with large behinds and fawn tweed caps, chased each other round a potted palm, shrieking appallingly.

"Simon, I don't see why you should wait."

"I said that I'd see you off, and I'm going to."

"But why?" I looked at him rather desperately. "The tender will probably be later than they say, and you may miss your train. And Hilda will have dinner waiting for you."

"Damn Hilda."

Two clergymen came and sat down on a spurious *petit point* sofa behind us.

"Only an extrahdinary act of Providence prevented me frahm sailing on the *Titanic*'s last voyage," said one.

"Ryally? What a tragedah that was!"

"Ryally, terrible."

Facing us was a rack of telegrams, flimsy little yellow messengers of death, of good fortune, of annoyance and comedy and despair. I stared at them and felt oppressed. It seemed stiflingly hot. Marcus was nowhere to be seen. Half my mind attended mechanically to the meanderings of the soft, soapy clerical voices behind us; the other half fretted: "I'm miserable! I hate this. What made the damn boat so late?" Fog was the answer, but I felt that it had a personal spite against me. This was not the large, splendid gesture of getting away from everything that I had planned. Instead of feeling free I was settling down slowly under a weight of depression. It was a mistake to have let Simon come.

I got up with sudden energy.

"Let's get out. It's not raining now. I hate this stuffy lounge."

There was a patch of blue sky and a strong salty wind. A steamer went "Wham! Wham!" Simon drew a deep breath.

"You're right. It was bloody awful in there."

"What shall we do?"

"We might take a tram ride as far as they go."

We climbed on top of the tram and away it snorted. A queer constraint was on us. We hardly said a word, but in some way all my perceptions were tremendously acute so that I took in everything that was going on in the streets. A shopping crowd surged over the pavements. In the windows were gaping carcases of meat, books, piles of vegetable marrows, terrible straw hats marked 6/11d. I thought vaguely: "Who buys all the terrible things in the world? Artificial flowers and nasty little brooches of Sealyhams in bad paste, and clothes-brushes, shaped like Micky the Mouse, and scarves worked in raffia?" A lovely, anaemic-looking girl stood on the kerb, anxiously tapping an envelope against her front teeth. Should she? Shouldn't she? And suddenly, having made her decision, all the interest went out of her face and she was just one of the cow-like millions who were trying to look like Greta Garbo.

We were reflected in the upper windows of the shops as we careered along, alone on the pitching, tossing deck of the tram. But a turn brought us among the meek little houses, the suburban heights of Southampton, and there were the pink casement curtains, "The Lilacs" and a dejected shrub that never burst out in gorgeous purple tubes of blossom; "Beethoven Villa," and a gramophone playing "Sonny Boy."

"Who do you suppose wants to live in Southampton, Simon?"

He asked:

"Do you know that Marcus Chard is in love with you?"

We had come to the truncating of the tram-lines, the ultimate end of all things. The conductor ran upstairs, jingling briskly, seized the electric arm of the tram and reversed it with a clang. The sun came out in a burst, a gush of brightness.

"Yes."

And off we clattered again past "The Lilacs" and "Beethoven Villa." I was filled with surprise at my own answer, which must have been in my head for a long time without my knowing it, and then I was interested and thought: "It's like a scene out of *Tchehov!*" Simon and I, swaying about in the cold, salty air, our bodies touching; the sparse dialogue.

"Do you know? …"

"Yes."

It reminded me of that bit in *The Duel* where Laevsky discovers that Nadyezhda Fyodorovna has been unfaithful to him.

"Is it you? Is the storm over?"

"Yes."

She remembered; put both her hands to her head and shuddered all over.

"How miserable I am!" she said.

We were back in the town and neither of us had spoken a word. There were still hours of time to kill. We got off the tram.

"What next?"

"We could go to a cinema."

"All right."

The posters said "Lili Kasteliz in Misfit Wives." I thought of goldfish-coloured hair and liquid dark eyes; a perfect bosom calling attention to itself through thin white crêpe. "*Je suis très internationale.*" I laughed. Once, for five seconds, I had been furiously jealous of Lili.

"Did you ever take her to lunch at Quaglino's, Simon?"

"Oh, my God!" said Simon, "that awful woman!"

We plunged into darkness, and there she was? several times over life-size, and there, too, was the bosom, more insecurely covered than ever. A woman's voice whispered excitably behind us:

"She's a degenerate little bitch, I bet."

"S-sh! Shut up, Daisy!"

"Well, she *looks* it. ..."

I sat watching Lili and tried to realise that in a few hours I should be on a ship moving inexorably away over two thousand miles of water. The darkness was warm and friendly, smelling of dusty plush and tobacco and human bodies that were sweating a little as they watched maiden virtue rudely strumpeted. Subtitle: "Stay for to-night, and to-morrow—we'll talk business!" But the sweating is unnecessary. No one really believes that Lili's virtue is going to be strumpeted, yet hope springs eternal. They lean forward, clammy hands gripping. Ah, there she goes! "If you don't open that door, Count, I'll ring the bell and my servants will throw you out." That's the stuff!

Simon stirred beside me.

"What are you going to do about it?"

And I understood, somehow, that he had gone back to the conversation on the tram.

"I don't know."

The lights went up. I looked sideways at Simon; he was sitting low down his seat, eyelids sagging. His profile seemed extraordinarily clean-cut in this warm, indefinite haze of tobacco-smoke and muddled colours. He looked very fair. But I had the strangest feeling that this was none of the Simons I knew. Four years were wiped out and I was face to face with a baffling stranger whose inner mind ...

"What are you thinking, Simon?"

And, without turning, he said:

"I was wondering how long it would be before you were Chard's mistress."

The lights went down, and towards us streamed someone launching a battleship; someone getting into an aeroplane and showing discoloured teeth; someone sending East End mothers off for a lovely fortnight in the country.

❧

It was very cold on the tender and there was a wicked roll. I felt that if I went downstairs I should be sick, so we stayed on deck, wrapped in rugs. It was almost dark. Above the horizon there was a rim of pure, luminous white, and against it drifted a long, purple-grey cloud. It kept on changing its shape. Now it was a ship, now a woman lying propped on her elbow, and suddenly it dissolved entirely; it floated away in vague, smoke-like wisps, and presently a skim of darkness closed over the luminous sky.

Simon asked: "Are you cold?"

"No." But then I said hastily: "Yes. Come and sit down beside me. You'll keep off the wind."

He sat down. I felt his warm body through the tweed of my new coat, and suddenly I was lonely and afraid.

"Simon—"

"Yes?"

"Poor Hilda, keeping your dinner!"

"It doesn't matter. I'll have something when I get back to Southampton."

"Mind you do."

He said suddenly:

"There's Marcus."

I did not look round. I did not want Marcus to see me. I had a queer feeling that if I looked into his face I should find out some dreadful truth about him and myself and life. It was eerie, ploughing along through the darkening water towards the great ship that waited for us, invisible in the darkness. I pressed against Simon.

"Has he gone?"

"Yes, he's gone downstairs. Looking for you, probably."

"Is he alone?"

"No, there's a man with him."

We were silent. Out of the darkness floated a soapy clerical voice:

"He put up a particulah fine pahformance playing at Lord's in 'eighty-seven—"

"Simon—"

"Yes?"

"Are you angry with me?"

"No, I'm not angry."

"Everything's been so beastly lately. Gwen dying and—everything. I want to get away for a bit and think and work. That's all it is."

"I know."

Suddenly there were lights glittering through the darkness; first a vague blur and then a solid wall of lights.

"There she is."

We stood up. All round us was an expectant bustle of departure; people jammed us in a solid block, craning their necks to see the ship and frenziedly calling names. I slipped my hand in the pocket of Simon's coat and found his hand.

"You'll write, won't you, Simon?"

"My letters are so damn bad. You won't be able to read them, anyway."

"Never mind. Write!"

I gave a funny laugh. Someone rammed a dressing-case into my back. "Oh, pardon *me*! Edith, is Junior with you? E-dith!" The iron wall of the ship loomed over us. Now we could see a square of light and some ship's officers waiting in the square. A gang-plank rattled, and a rope flexed out like a snake.

"Hilda will look after you all right."

"Oh, I'll manage. Don't you worry."

"Will you explain when you see your mother that—"

The crowd was moving. One by one they tramped up the gangway, turning resolute faces towards the light, and disappeared into the bowels of the ship. There was something very Old Testament about it. They might have been the Chosen People crossing the Red Sea, clasping their little bundles, pathetic and intrepid dots against the night. And the awful, inexorable strength of the ship crushed me. It condemned me to departure as relentlessly as death. When I walked up that gangway I should lose my identity and become just an anonymous dot in the grip of an iron monster; a printed name in the passenger-list; a cow that had to be bundled into a cattle-wagon and transported somewhere, indifferently.

Warmth and brightness; the tramp of feet on decks. People were running up and down as though they were in a shipwreck.

"What's the number of your cabin?"

I searched for my tickets and told him.

"You ought to be on Deck B. Come along."

We walked up the narrow passage between the little white doors. A stout woman popped her head out and popped back again like a water-rat. Coming from the cold air it seemed stiflingly hot. Simon flung open a door.

"Here we are."

"Yes."

"Quite a nice bathroom."

"Yes." I wanted to run, burst into tears, hammer my two fists against something. "It's hot down here."

"I'll open a porthole."

He struggled with it, breathing hard. I stood in the middle of the floor and watched him. And suddenly I seemed to realise that he was going away; that in a few minutes he would get on the tender, and the tender would vanish into the darkness and

I should be alone. I felt such an appalling rush of pain that it was almost physical, and through my head rushed the thought: "Now I know what they mean about being one flesh." For it was as though a living, breathing part of my flesh was being torn violently away; there was the stab of a knife, and my heart and guts seemed to gush out. My throat ached with tears. I must have made some sort of sound.

Simon looked round from the porthole. And suddenly, violently, we were in each other's arms; our bodies were pressed together as though nothing would ever get them apart. His lips were hard, and hurt me. There was a salty taste on them.

I looked up, and Simon was crying; the tears were running down his cheeks. I kept on saying foolishly:

"I'll come back. Oh, my love, my darling, don't mind so much. I'll come back."

"You'll never come back."

He kissed me with a sort of despairing violence, and then, quite suddenly, let me go. The door banged. I screamed: "Simon!"

Time passed. Footsteps passed and re-passed the door; a voice called something in French. I dragged myself up, washed my face in cold water and pulled a comb through my hair with nervous haste. My face was terrible. I thought: "Who cares?"

It was cold on deck and almost deserted. Only a few people were gathered at the side, looking down at the last bits of luggage being unloaded from the tender. I pushed my way among them. They looked at me curiously. Simon was walking about the deck, his hands in his pocket, not looking up. I steadied my voice and shouted:

"Simon!"

The wind caught my voice and threw it sportively away. I thought desperately, "Oh, God, help me!" and again I shouted:

"Simon! Coo-ee! Simon!"

He looked up. I tried to arrange my trembling face into some sort of smile.

"Good-bye, Simon!"

Faintly his voice floated up. "Good-bye, Nevis!" The tender began to edge fussily away from the parent boat; there were shouts; a rope struck the water. Now I can see his light overcoat. He is waving. Now the darkness is swallowing them up and he's just a vague shape, an indefinite waving blot. "Good-bye, Simon!" I can't see anything. ... I can't see anything. ...

The other people had melted away. I still stood there, looking out into the darkness, thinking that I could hear the tender above the noise of the waves and wind. The tears were running down my face. I did not try to stop them.

"I'll come back. I'll come back, Simon!"

"You'll never come back."

And suddenly I knew what he must have known all along. I knew that Marcus was in love with me and would try to make love to me. I knew that he did not care a damn about my books. I knew that one day I would let him be my lover, because I was silly and shallow and vain, and things would happen that way. I said aloud "No!" but the sea, sighing beneath me, seemed to answer with a little hiss: Yes—yes-s—yes-s-s!

The ship began to thud and vibrate. In a few minutes we should be moving. All sorts of pictures seemed to form against the darkness. Simon lying asleep in that cold crystalline dawn among the pines; Simon saying "Why the hell do you put that muck on your face?" Simon, a beautiful brown savage lying in the sun; Simon in that funny little country room over a weir.

> Do you remember an Inn, Miranda?
> Do you remember an Inn? …
> No sound but the boom
> Of the far waterfall like Doom.

Boom—doom—boom—went the ship's engines. There were shouts, there was a tremendous thudding noise, and we began to move. Foam spurted up from the dark green water. Silently and mysteriously the reflected lights crept from wave to wave.

I stayed against the rail, looking up at the sky. It was not foggy now. The night was bright and calm; there was one large star hanging directly ahead. It seemed to look down on me, the sea, the silently-moving ship, with a calm ironic twinkle. "Well! What are you going to do next?"

I looked out into the darkness and repeated:

"I'll come back."

The star was still there. Its brightness seemed to comfort me. But suddenly it vanished behind a cloud.

New York, 1930.

✵ ✵ ✵

Afterword

✵

If you opened the first edition of *My Husband Simon*, published by The Literary Press in 1931, the first words you'd find would be a section called 'This is the Story' opposite the title page. It's only a paragraph, designed to give the 1930s reader a sense of whether they'd want to read the book. And this is what, according to this paragraph, is 'the Story':

My Husband Simon tells the story of the married life of Nevis Falconer, a young woman novelist, and Simon Quinn. Temperamentally unsuited, only a mutual physical attraction, sufficiently strong in itself, keeps them together in spite of innumerable quarrels. They live this superficial existence for three years, until one day Nevis meets Marcus Chard, her American publisher, who has just arrived in London. Soon friendship develops into Love. Inevitably the problem faces her. Wife or mistress? Nevis finds herself caught in a whirl of circumstances over which she has no control.

Allowing for a somewhat casual approach to sentence structure and the use of capital letters, this is broadly what happens in Mollie Panter-Downes' third novel, but it still feels like an inadequate description. The plot is engaging and the novel certainly makes for compelling reading, but surprisingly little takes place. It is mostly a portrait of an incompatible marriage, told with Panter-Downes' lightness of touch even while there is an underlying tragedy. Readers waiting for the problem of 'wife or mistress?' to face Nevis will, indeed, be waiting an awfully long time. When Marcus does make his intentions clear, and the choice is before Nevis, it is really only the manifestation of the ongoing difficulty of her marriage: class.

Class distinctions were certainly not a new thing in the period between the World Wars; in England, they could lay claim to being the dominant feature of all social arrangements throughout the nation's history. But in this period – as Nicola Humble suggests in her book *The Feminine Middlebrow Novel 1920s to 1950s* – the middle class was becoming increasingly self-conscious. This meant not only defining what it was to be middle class, but also what it wasn't. In truth, Nevis and Simon are both middle class – she is upper-middle and he lower-middle (working in cigarette advertising). Their proximity on the social scale makes their differences all the clearer.

Simon's 'idea of real enjoyment was sitting in a hot, crowded tap-room, talking horses with a drunk navvy who might later try to pick a fight with him'. Nevis, meanwhile, is dismissive of 'women who made fumbling, ineffectual gestures and said "Pardon!" when they committed a social error'. Twenty years later, Nancy Mitford would popularise the terms 'U' and 'non-U', where 'U' stood for 'upper class': 'U' people would use words such as *napkin*, *what?*, and *sofa*, while the non-U would opt for *serviette*, *pardon?*, and *settee*. In the 1930s, this battle was played out equally between different echelons of the middle class.

There were many prisms through which class was codified and understood in this period, and a lot could certainly be said about vocabulary, dress, occupation, politics and myriad other lines along which a class divide could be identified. In *My Husband Simon*, and in the 1930s more generally, it is often done through literature.

The first words that Simon says to Nevis are an acknowledgement that he has not read her book – Nevis has published a bestseller as a teenager, as Panter-Downes had herself with *The Shoreless Sea* in 1923.

"I wish that I could say I'd read your book."

"Why should you?"

"Well, it would make a good beginning. But, as a matter of fact, I don't read anything. I'm practically illiterate."

He made the statement with an irritating satisfaction.

Mass literacy was one of the major factors shifting understanding of class in the twentieth century - John Carey wrote in *The Intellectuals and the Masses* that 'the difference between the nineteenth-century mob and the twentieth-century mass is literacy' – but anti-intellectualism became a badge of honour for many in the period. Indeed, Nevis does not think her husband at all intelligent, but according to Simon, she 'damned anyone as unintelligent who (a) had not seen the latest play and read the latest novel; (b) did not know who Virginia Woolf was; (c) could not look at a dress and say, "My dear, is it Molyneux?"'. Woolf was alive and writing when *My Husband Simon* was published, and had published some of her most noted novels (*Mrs Dalloway*, *To The Lighthouse*, *Orlando*) in the previous five years. She had yet to write the novel that sold the most during her lifetime, *The Years*.

Of course, class and education are not identical, and we shouldn't assume that everybody from the upper-middle class understood one set of references that was missed by the lower-middle class (Simon's 'cheerful, rather common' father, for instance, reads the curious trio of Leo Tolstoy, Thomas de Quincey, and G.K. Chesterton). Equally, readers could not be expected to stick solely to the category of literature for which they were deemed eligible. But these sorts of classifications helped designate not only which authors belonged in which categories, but which readers could congregate, too. Certainly, Nevis sees her taste in (and knowledge of) literature as setting her apart from her husband and his family.

One of the first literary allusions that Nevis almost makes, but decides not to, becomes a recurring image in the novel: 'Do you remember an Inn, Miranda? / Do you remember an Inn?' The lines are from Hilaire Belloc's poem 'Tarantella', which had only been published in 1929 – indeed, as the scene where Nevis recalls it is apparently set in 1926, four years before the main events of the novel, the poem had yet to be written. This error aside, it is indicative of her immediate understanding of Simon that she decides not to make the reference, as 'of course Simon didn't read Belloc'.

Literary allusions could be a codeword to people within a certain group, and the failure of the listener to recognise them marked them as an outsider. This could cause embarrassment to the one who made the allusion, of course. In E.M. Delafield's popular and amusing *Diary of a Provincial Lady*, published the previous year, the narrator is reminded of *Jane Eyre* by eating burnt porridge, but when she says this to her husband Robert, 'this literary allusion not a success'. The unnamed Provincial Lady often makes similar references to the sorts of books the reader is expected to love (*Little Women*, Dickens) and they are seldom met with anything but appalled confusion from other characters.

The antagonism caused by these literary divides is put into a fairly crude concrete form in *My Husband Simon* when Nevis recollects, 'once I threw a book of Eugene O'Neill's plays at him and nicked a bit off the side of his forehead'.

Like O'Neill, the reputation of some of the authors used to classify people have survived to the twenty-first century. Others, and their connotations, are rather more faded. Simon's mother is placed, in Nevis's mind, by her affection of Michael Arlen, Stephen McKenna, and the 'such nice stories' of Warwick Deeping. All three wrote bestsellers in the 1920s, often focusing on class; all three were usually dismissed by gatekeepers of high literary culture at the time. Mrs Quinn is similarly dismissed by Nevis. Indeed, she decides that the surname 'symbolise[s] a whole class of society' – one not characterised by wealth but by aesthetic judgement:

London was full of Quinns, eating saddle of mutton at handsome mahogany tables; going up the steps of good clubs and stepping out of quiet, expensive cars; thinking that 'art' meant the Royal Academy, and 'beauty' was the sort of wishy-washy, rubber-stamp, damnable prettiness that you see on the lid of a chocolate-box.

Many of the books used as signposts in this way were published only shortly before *My Husband Simon* itself. Nevis mentions Vita Sackville-West's *The Edwardians* – a bestseller published in 1930 by Leonard and Virginia Woolf's Hogarth Press – and Aldous Huxley's 1924 collection of short stories *Little Mexican*.

Nevis also refers to a cause célèbre of the period, D.H. Lawrence's *Lady Chatterley's Lover* – 'I think that I wanted to see copies of *Lady Chatterley's Lover* distributed free to everyone over the age of fourteen. It was true that Lawrence was one of my gods, but I rather overdid things'. *Lady Chatterley's Lover* had been privately published (in Italy) in 1928 and in 1929 in France and Australia, and was notorious in its day. Banned in the UK for another three decades, it could only be read in an expurgated version or by acquiring an illicit copy. Those who didn't read it at the time might not be choosing to avoid it out of moral outrage; like Delafield's Provincial Lady, they might simply want to avoid the inconvenience: 'I ask unknown lady on my right if it can be got from the Times Book Club, and she says No, only in Paris, and advises me to go there before I return home. Cannot, however, feel that grave additional expense thus incurred would be justified'.

As another novel depicting a romance across a class divide, *Lady Chatterley's Lover* makes for an interesting comparison with *My Husband Simon* – if only for the fact it is about the only similarity between the two novels. Despite originally being published as *Nothing In Common But Sex* in America, *My Husband Simon* is emphatically not a man's sexual fantasy of bridging the class divide. Simon and Nevis are both virgins at the outset of the novel, and there is far less disparity in their social echelons than between Lady Chatterley and Oliver Mellors.

One of the most interesting elements in *My Husband Simon* is Nevis's career as a writer. It is unclear how autobiographical these sections are, but perhaps we can see glimmers of Panter-Downes' own experience of writing a bestseller, following it up with a less successful novel, and then trying to establish where she fits in the literary canon. We can only imagine the full contents of *The Forcing House* and *Vulcan Harvest*.

Nevis does frivolously mention that she wants to 'write a strong, earthy book that will win the Femina Prize'. The Femina – Vie Heureuse Prize was set up in 1920 as an English equivalent of the French Prix Femina (created in 1904). In the twenty years that the prize existed, winners ranged from Woolf's *To the Lighthouse* and E.M. Forster's *A Passage to India* to *Precious Bane* by Mary Webb and *Gallion's Reach* by H.M. Tomlinson. Some of the award winners' names are now probably familiar only to a handful of readers: Bradda Field, Constance Holmes, Gordon Bottomley. It's unclear whether Nevis Quinn is of the same literary calibre to find her name on the list. But it is literature that ultimately spells the probable end of Nevis and Simon's marriage. Marcus steps in with his literary knowledge and, as Simon says when he realises they will sail away together: "You like him, don't you? He can talk books and all the rest of it. He understands you."

Panter-Downes' later masterpiece, 1947's *One Fine Day*, is

※ ※ ※

class conscious but makes steps towards egalitarianism in its heroine's musings on the impacts of war on everybody in her village. *My Husband Simon* considers class in a different way, suggesting that love, or at least attraction, may not be quite enough to overcome the everyday obstacles that arose in 1930 from the meeting of two people who were just slightly too far apart on the nebulous but keenly felt social spectrum. As the novel closes, Nevis is reminded again of Belloc's 'Tarantella', thinking of 'No sound but the boom / Of the far waterfall like Doom'. Some sort of doom is on her mind but, of course, Simon wouldn't understand the reference.

Simon Thomas

Series consultant **Simon Thomas** created the middlebrow blog Stuck in a Book in 2007. He is also the co-host of the popular podcast Tea or Books? Simon has a PhD from Oxford University in Interwar Literature.